PUFFIN BOOKS
VICTORY SONG

Chitra Banerjee Divakaruni is an award-winning author and poet. Her work has been published in over fifty magazines, including the *Atlantic Monthly* and the *New Yorker*, and her writing has been included in over sixty anthologies. Her works have been translated into fourteen languages, including Dutch, Hebrew and Japanese. Her other children's books are *The Conch Bearer* and *The Mirror of Fire and Dreaming*. Her novel, *The Mistress of Spices*, was made into a movie. She lives in Houston with her husband and two sons, and teaches at the University of Houston.

GW00601950

Victory Song

Chitra Banerjee Divakaruni

PUFFIN BOOKS

PUFFIN BOOKS
Published by the Penguin Group
Penguin Books India Pvt. Ltd, 11 Community Centre, Panchsheel Park, New Delhi
110 017, India
Penguin Group (USA) Inc., 375 Hudson Street, New York, New York 10014, USA
Penguin Group (Canada), 90 Eglinton Avenue East, Suite 700, Toronto, Ontario,
M4P 2Y3, Canada (a division of Pearson Penguin Canada Inc.)
Penguin Books Ltd, 80 Strand, London WC2R 0RL, England
Penguin Ireland, 25 St Stephen's Green, Dublin 2, Ireland (a division of Penguin
Books Ltd)
Penguin Group (Australia), 250 Camberwell Road, Camberwell, Victoria 3124,
Australia (a division of Pearson Australia Group Pty Ltd)
Penguin Group (NZ), 67 Apollo Drive, Rosedale, North Shore 0632, New Zealand
(a division of Pearson New Zealand Ltd)
Penguin Group (South Africa) (Pty) Ltd, 24 Sturdee Avenue, Rosebank, Johannesburg
2196, South Africa

Penguin Books Ltd, Registered Offices: 80 Strand, London WC2R 0RL, England

First published in Puffin by Penguin Books India 2006

Copyright © Chitra Banerjee Divakaruni 2006

The right of Chitra Banerjee Divakaruni to be identified as the author of this work
has been asserted by her in accordance with the Copyright, Designs and Patents Act
1988.

ISBN-13: 978-0-14333-019-6   ISBN-10: 0-14333-019-5

This is a work of fiction. Names, characters, places and incidents are either the
product of the author's imagination or are used fictitiously, and any resemblance to
any actual person, living or dead, events or locales is entirely coincidental.

Typeset in Sabon by Mantra Virtual Services, New Delhi
Printed at DeUnique Printers, New Delhi

For my favourite young people:

Abhay, Anand, Rahul and Neela

Contents

Acknowledgements

My thanks to:

My spiritual teachers, Baba Muktananda, Gurumayi, and Swami Chinamayananda, for their love. My agent, Sandra Dijkstra, for encouraging me to grow in this new and joyous direction. My editor, Tamara England, for her perceptive guidance. My mother, Tatini Banerjee, for making the time I write about here come alive for me. My friend, Indira Chakravorty, for generously sharing with me her extensive library of Bengali literature. My husband, Murthy, for his continued support. My niece, Neela, for loaning me her name and my son, Anand, for being my first, best, and most enthusiastic reader.

Author's Note

When I was writing Neela's story, I read about India's freedom movement and talked to people who lived through it—including my mother. In fact, I couldn't have imagined the characters and the world of *Victory Song* without her help. She is blessed with a great memory and gave me many wonderful details. She told me of growing up in a village and of going to a women's college in Calcutta in the late 1930s. She patiently answered all my questions—from what a village wedding would have been like to what kinds of underwear girls wore! She described life in Calcutta, a centre of India's independence movement, in vivid detail.

I had long been fascinated with two of the great leaders of the day, Mohandas Gandhi and Subhash Bose, men whose goals were the same but whose paths were so different: Gandhi believed in non-violence to overcome Britain, while Bose sought victory by any means necessary—including violence. These men and the British rulers are the only historical figures in the story. All the other characters came from my imagination.

Because I grew up in Calcutta, I know that city well, although it has changed much since Neela's time. And Neela's village is based on my own ancestral village, which *hasn't* changed much—except that it now has running water, electricity, and a girls' school.

To get a sense of Neela's daily life—what people wore and ate and how they thought—I read Bengali novels of the 1930s by Sharat Chandra and Tagore, and an earlier novel by Bankim Chandra, who composed *Vande Mataram*, the song that inspired Neela and the entire nation. Bengali is my mother tongue, so I read these writers in the original, enjoying the flavour and sound of the words, some of which I've put into *Victory Song*. All three authors wrote about the lives of girls and women, describing how they received little education and often were expected to stay home and care for the household. Some of the impatience I felt reading these descriptions found its way into Neela's character. I chose the name 'Neela' because in Bengali, it means 'blue', a colour that symbolizes infinite possibilities—both for Neela herself and for India.

Wedding Preparations

'Girls! Get up! Have you forgotten what day it is!'

Neela awoke with a start at the sound of her mother's voice. She had been deep in a dream, a beautiful dream about a lovely woman with hair like waves and a crown of diamonds on her head and sad, sad eyes. The dream had been so real that for a moment Neela blinked with sleepy confusion at her mother, who stood at the door of the bedroom Neela shared with her older sister, Usha. Ma looked pretty in a new yellow sari, but she looked a bit harried as well.

'Come on, Neela, get dressed quickly. I need your help with setting out things for the turmeric bath ceremony. And Usha, my dear, you need to wash up and change into your yellow sari. The guests will be arriving soon.'

Excitement flooded through Neela as it all came back to her. Of course! Today was Usha's wedding day! Preparations would begin in just a little while with gaye halud, a ritual where the women of the village would pour turmeric water over Usha's head for good luck. Turmeric water made a terrible yellow mess—that's why the women had to be dressed in yellow, too. *Ugh!* thought Neela, glad that all she had to do with the ceremony was to put out the trays that would hold the necessary good luck items, such as a lamp, betel leaves, a conch shell, and flowers.

'Don't be late,' their mother warned them. Her sari rustling, she started for the backyard, where large fire pits had been constructed for the wedding cooking. The women would be staying for lunch. It would be quite a spread—wedding meals always were—with the best basmati rice, five kinds of vegetable curries, an elaborate kurma made from fish caught just this morning from their own pond, and two kinds of dessert. But this was a comparatively simple meal. The real feast would be tonight, after the wedding, when more than one hundred guests from several of the surrounding villages were expected.

Neela had heard her parents discussing it a few weeks ago.

'We should keep it small, Sarada,' her father, Hari Charan, had said thoughtfully. 'It's a difficult time, not a time for celebration. Another war has started in Europe.'

'But what does a war in Europe have to do with us?' Neela's mother asked impatiently.

'There are troubles here, too,' he said. 'So many people, both young and old, have taken up the struggle for India's independence. They're risking their lives each day for the sake of our country.'

'But this is the first wedding in our family!' Sarada had exclaimed, agitated. Neela knew how much her mother had been looking forward to it.

Hari Charan still looked worried. 'So many farmers—especially the cotton growers—have been suffering since the British started importing machine-spun thread from Manchester, which is what the cloth mills prefer. We're lucky because I grow rice, which has been fetching a steady price, but many people don't even have enough to eat. It's no wonder the countryside is overrun by bands of robbers! It doesn't seem right to have a lavish wedding right now.'

Neela had a feeling that her father was right, but her mother wouldn't give in. 'I know times are hard, and I sympathize with the poor,' she said. 'Don't I give food to every beggar who shows up on our doorstep? But what would people say if the oldest daughter of Hari Charan Sen, the most successful farmer in all of Shona Gram, were married off like a beggar girl, with only a handful of people to wish her well? I was hoping to invite two hundred people, and to hire a band from Calcutta to play the wedding music, like at the marriage of Ram Prasad Chowdhury's son.'

'I'm not the most successful farmer in the village,' Hari Charan had said in his reasonable voice, 'though by God's grace, our new fertilizer mix has worked out well. Besides, Ram Prasad Chowdhury is the zamindar of the village. His ancestors used to own all the land around here—remember? They were like kings. It's silly to think of competing with him. We can get a shehnai player from Bardhaman, but that's about it.'

'We can't go lower than a hundred people, that much

is certain,' Sarada had said in her firmest tone, the one Neela knew well. 'Otherwise Usha would be terribly disappointed.'

Neela glanced at the wooden cot, the exact replica of her own, where her older sister slept. Usually Usha, who loved to sleep, would be burrowed under the sheets, with a pillow covering her face. But today she was already awake. She stared up at the wooden beams of the ceiling, chewing nervously on her lip. Neela had been excited about her sister's marriage. Apart from all the fun and games that were usual at a wedding, Neela would finally have a room to herself. But now she felt a guilty pang. She went over to Usha and gave her a hug.

'Don't worry, Didi,' she said. 'Everything will be fine— as long as you don't trip on your sari when going around the wedding fire!'

'But Neela, I don't know him at all. What if he doesn't like me after we're married? What if none of his family likes me?' Usha's voice sounded tearful and much younger than her fifteen years.

By *him* she meant Gopal, her husband-to-be, the son of another affluent farmer who lived three villages away. The marriage had been arranged last month, after Gopal and his family, along with the village matchmaker, came to see Usha. Gopal was good-looking and had a pleasant smile, and from time to time Neela had caught him glancing with shy interest at her sister. But she understood Usha's fears. And yet—that's how it always had been in traditional Indian families like theirs. Young men and women weren't allowed to meet alone and get to know each other, not even after their weddings had been arranged. And the thought of choosing one's own husband was, of course, out of the question.

Neela sighed. *But why can't a girl choose her own husband?* she thought. *What's wrong with that?* Then she shook her head with a smile. *Silly girl!* she said to herself. *You're only twelve years old. You don't need to worry about a husband for years and years.*

'I'm quite sure he likes you, Didi,' she said to Usha. 'His whole family does—or they wouldn't have chosen you, would they? You're so pretty and sweet-natured, you'll get along great with them!' Neela knew in her heart this was true. Usha was petite and fair-skinned, with long black hair and thick black eyelashes. She was also quiet and obedient, as their mother was often fond of pointing out.

'Neela!' her mother would say, shaking her head, when her younger daughter came in with a scraped knee from climbing a tree or with her dress muddy from having given a bath to Budhi, her favourite cow. 'Look at you! Thin as a stick of bamboo from running around so much. And getting darker each day from being out in the sun. No one will want to marry you when the time comes. Why can't you be more like Didi, and sit calmly at home with a piece of embroidery, as girls should!' Then she'd glance accusingly at her husband. 'It's because you spoil her,' she'd say.

Hari Charan would smile indulgently. 'My Neela's a smart girl. Didn't you hear what the pandit said last week, when he came over for the girls' lessons? She reads and writes better than any girl her age that he knows—better than her sister, even.'

Neela had felt proud to hear her father say that.

'Yes, but what good will that do her, except fill her head with too many strange ideas?' Sarada had asked with a sigh. 'I can barely read, but I've done just fine, haven't I? Usha can sew and embroider. She knows how to make mango pickles and sweet rasagollas. That's what prospective in-laws look for in girls.'

Neela knew that what her mother said was true—that was what people wanted in a daughter-in-law. But weren't other things important, too?

'Don't worry, Sarada!' her father had said with a laugh. 'Our Neela sings so beautifully, she'll charm them all.'

A voice broke into Neela's thoughts. 'Usha! Neela! Aren't you ready yet?'

'Oh dear, there's Ma calling,' Neela said, nudging her sister. 'You'd better hurry. And anytime you feel scared, just think of your wedding outfit and all that lovely jewellery you'll be wearing tonight.'

Neela had said the right thing. Usha's face lit up. Neela knew that Usha loved dressing in fancy clothes and that she loved her wedding sari. It was a beautiful red Benarasi silk embroidered with gold thread. Hari Charan had made a special trip to the famous Sialdah Bazaar in Calcutta to buy it. There was a fine red petticoat of the softest cotton to wear under it, and an elbow-length brocade blouse with frilled sleeves. Usha picked up her clothes from the wooden alna where her mother had hung them last night and wandered off toward the washroom with a dreamy smile.

Neela pulled on a fresh shift, baggy drawers, and a clean frock that reached past her knees. Normally she was considered too young to wear a sari, for which she was thankful. She didn't know how she would ever manage the six yards of material a sari was made of! It would put an end to tree climbing and swimming across the pond for sure! But tonight at the wedding she would wear her first one, and she quite looked forward to it. Her sari, too, had been bought at the Sialdah Bazaar, and it was a beautiful deep orange silk embroidered with a silver paisley design. The shopkeeper had told her father this style was all the rage in Calcutta.

Neela walked out to the porch, where her family's maid had placed a bowlful of the freshly cut neem sticks that the family used to brush their teeth. She grabbed one and made for the pump. She chewed on the slightly bitter stick as she went. She pumped a bucket of cool water, washed her face, and was about to visit the outhouse when she heard a loud, angry mooing coming all the way from the cow barn.

It was Budhi! It was time for her to be milked, yes, but she usually waited patiently for Neela to come to her. Something else must have upset her.

Neela hurried toward the barn—and straight into

Great-aunt Mangala, who was here for the wedding. Neela's great-aunt had been coming around the corner of the house with an armload of mango leaves, with which the wedding area was to be decorated. The mango leaves fell to the ground, and Neela bent to pick them up.

'And where do you think you're dancing off to, young lady?' Great-aunt asked with a scowl, once she got back her breath. 'Didn't your mother ask you to come and help her?'

'I'll be back right away,' Neela said, 'as soon as I take care of Budhi.'

'You don't need to run after that cow anymore. I sent Haru, the new servant boy, to milk her. It isn't proper for you, a grown girl from a good family, to be hanging around in the cow barn.'

'But Great-aunt—' Neela started. Then she broke off. Budhi's mooing was louder than before, and Neela could hear clanking sounds. It was no use trying to explain to Great-aunt that Budhi didn't like anyone except Neela handling her—and that's the way it had been since Budhi was a calf and her father had given her to Neela as a birthday gift.

Neela slipped away and ran off toward the barn with Great-aunt's shouts echoing behind her.

'Wait till I tell your mother! You have no respect for elders! None at all!'

Neela grimaced. She hoped her mother would be more understanding.

The barn was a long, low structure built of mud and brick, with small windows that let in only a little light.

Against one wall were stacks of hay. The buffaloes had already been taken to till the fields, but the cows were still tethered in their stalls—all except for Budhi, that is. She had broken her rope, knocked over her milking pail, and was mooing and shaking her horns fiercely at Haru, who had backed up against a wall and was on the verge of tears.

Neela sighed. Any other servant would have known better than to try to milk her cow. 'Budhi!' she called sternly, and when the cow turned, Neela caught hold of her rope and signalled to the boy to go—which he quickly did. Neela began to calm Budhi, laying her face against the cow's back and stroking the loose, soft skin under her neck. 'That's my good girl,' she whispered, 'my little jewel!' It was what her father called Neela when he hugged her good night.

Budhi mooed accusingly at her mistress, as though asking how Neela could have betrayed her like this, but then she quieted down a little and allowed Neela to tether her again.

The cow was still too upset for her milk to flow properly, so Neela sang her a song about cows at harvest time and rubbed her back. Neela's voice, clear as a temple bell, rose to the rafters of the barn. Budhi nuzzled Neela, pleased.

'You're my most appreciative audience, aren't you?' Neela laughed. 'But you'd better let me milk you fast today. Ma's probably mad at me already.'

Neela was right. By the time she got back to the house with a full pail of milk, the village women had started arriving. A couple of them were setting out the good luck items—which she was to have done, Neela remembered guiltily. Her mother glared at her. 'I'll deal with you later,' she said sharply. 'Go change your frock—there's dirt all along the hem.'

Neela felt bad. It was an important day, and her mother was anxious already. Neela hadn't meant to disobey her mother—but, on the other hand, she couldn't have just left Budhi like that, could she? Life was complicated, with duties that sometimes collided against each other. She would ask her father about it after the wedding was over and things were quiet again.

Meanwhile, she tried to make up for her behaviour by being extra helpful, fetching and carrying things, and greeting all the guests politely. At lunchtime, she set out the banana leaves on which everyone ate. Even though she was starving—she hadn't had a chance to eat breakfast—she helped her mother serve the guests first. And after the meal, Neela poured water for the women to wash their hands.

'What a good daughter you have here, Sarada,' said one of the women. 'It's obvious that you've brought her up well!'

Neela didn't recognize the speaker. This surprised her, because she knew all her mother's friends—and had known them for years. There wasn't much coming and going in her quiet little village, not among the women, at least. Once they got married, they stayed in their husbands' homes, with their in-laws, even if their husbands took jobs in nearby towns like Bardhaman or Dhanbad. Perhaps this woman was a relative of one of the other women? She looked like a pleasant person, with little laugh lines around her mouth. She was comfortably plump, and like the other women she wore a yellow cotton sari, but hers had a wide red border decorated with gold thread. There were stacks of thick gold bangles on her arms, which meant she was rich. When she spoke, a diamond winked merrily on her nose. Neela liked that, and she also liked the way her mother's face brightened with pleasure at the rare compliment about her troublesome second child. So Neela gave the woman her best smile before she went off to see how her sister was doing.

Neela lay on her cot impatiently in the warm afternoon, fanning herself with a palm-leaf fan. Sarada had decreed that both the girls were to rest until evening so that they would look their best for the wedding. Usha had not objected, and although she had tossed and turned nervously for a while, she had finally fallen asleep. But Neela, who was used to spending her afternoons on more useful activities—fishing at the pond with the new wheel rod her father let her use, or climbing the *jaam* tree to find the first ripe purple fruits—was wide awake and dead bored.

There wasn't even anything to read in the room.

'Resting does not mean straining your eyes reading all

that small print, young lady,' Great-aunt Mangala had said earlier when she had come to check on them. She had promptly confiscated the book Neela had been reading, a much-handled copy of the *Kathamala*, a book of animal fables that the pandit had loaned her the last time he came over for a lesson.

Neela had been annoyed. *Why does Great-aunt feel that she has the right to tell me what to do, just because she's older? It's not fair!* Neela thought. What was worse was that Mother would almost certainly side with Great-aunt if Neela were to complain. It was what Neela thought of as 'The Conspiracy of the Adults'.

Neela was doubly impatient because she had planned something quite different for this afternoon. She had planned to go to see the baoul.

The baoul was a wandering minstrel who turned up in the village from time to time. Neela was always happy to see him. For one thing, baouls were regarded as holy men. They wore saffron-coloured robes and gave up family ties and all other earthly goods, and their coming was supposed to bring a family good luck. But her baoul—that's how Neela thought of him—also knew what was going on in far-off, exciting places like Calcutta and Bombay, and he always had stories to tell. And though he was old and leaned on a staff when he walked, he still had a fine, clear voice and a large repertoire of songs. Neela would sit, mesmerized by his voice, as he sang of distant times and places and of gods and goddesses. He could even make everyday things, like a sunset, a storm, a harvest dance, or the fragrance of *kadam* flowers on a monsoon day, seem special. Each time he came, he taught Neela a song or two. It was the only musical instruction she ever received, there being no music teachers in their small village, and Neela waited for it thirstily.

The baoul had shown up at their home last night—appearing quite magically out of the darkness, Neela thought. Dinner had already been served by then. But a place had been quickly set for him with the other menfolk who had come from other villages and towns.

'What's the news, Baoul dadu?' Hari Charan had asked. That's what everyone in the village called him—dadu, or grandfather, to show respect. Neela, who had been sent from the kitchen with a plate of food for him, had listened avidly as the baoul spoke of the war that had started in Europe.

'It's a big war against Germany, bigger than any before. The Germans are dropping bombs from planes, blowing up cities. The British want India to help them fight Germany, like we did last time, twenty-some years back,' the baoul said. 'But our Congress leaders don't want to do it anymore. They say, "Why should our men die for Britain in some distant battlefield?"'

'That's right, why should they?' a man responded.

'But we're subjects of the King of England,' another said. 'The British are our rulers. They govern our country. Look at all the things they've given us—the courts, the railroads, good schools, secure jobs. We owe them our loyalty.'

'Nonsense!' someone shouted. 'The British have been looting us for over a hundred years. Don't you remember the indigo plantations, and how they forced our farmers to grow indigo so that they could sell the dye for a lot of money in Europe? What did we Indians ever get out of it?'

Other voices joined in heatedly. 'I heard they even stole the great diamond, the Koh-i-noor, that used to be in the palace of Delhi, and took it back to England, as though it were theirs . . .'

'But remember how things were before the British, with the nawabs and the maharajas? They didn't care for the people either. They did whatever they wanted, punishing anyone who disobeyed their whims, throwing peasants into dungeons or burying them alive, and taking their land. At least the British have fair laws—'

'Fair? You call them fair? Remember when they jailed Netaji Subhash Bose for demonstrating against them? They sent him all the way to Rangoon, to that dreadful prison, where he almost died, just because he stood up and said India should be independent—'

'I hear he's back again now and is urging people to defy the British,' Neela heard her father say.

'There are so many rumours nowadays, you never know whom to believe.'

'It's no rumour,' the baoul's voice broke in above the hubbub. 'He is back. His presence has given new strength to our freedom fighters. They're planning—'

But what they were planning Neela didn't get to hear, because at that moment her mother called her back to the kitchen and gave her a thorough scolding for standing there gawking among the menfolk, where she had no cause to be.

'But, Ma—' Neela started to say. 'You're growing too big to be sitting out there with the men,' her mother said. 'Didn't you notice that you're the only girl out there who's older than ten? And anyway, I need you to help me in the kitchen. Maybe then you'll learn some womanly skills.' But after Neela had helped her for a while, Ma relented. 'You can listen to the singing from behind the door, where the other women are sitting,' she said.

From behind the door, Neela couldn't see the baoul's face as he sang or the deft movements of his fingers dancing on the ektara's string, which she loved to watch. But at least she could hear.

'Here's a song so old that it has become new,' the baoul was saying. 'Many of you haven't heard it—it was banned by the British some years ago. But it's time for us to hear it again.' Then he started. '*Vande Mataram!*' he sang, 'Hail, motherland!'

> *Sashya shyamalam, malayaja sheetalam*
> *fulla kusumita*
> *mataram . . .*

His voice was deep and serious in places, high and joyous in others. He was describing India—their motherland—beautiful with her green fields, her cool breezes on a hot day, the sweet voices of her people. She was an ideal to be loved, a goddess to be admired, a cause to give up one's life for.

Neela creased her forehead, trying to understand the unfamiliar Bengali words from an older time. The baoul was asking the motherland for blessing, for the courage to fight to the death. His voice dipped, raw and sorrowful, as he sang.

Seventy million of us to raise our voices
against injustice,
One hundred forty million arms that could
raise their swords.
Why, then, are you still so helpless, Mother?

The verse made something electric go through Neela. Why, indeed, were they, a country of so many people, so helpless against a few thousand British? Looking at the women around her, she noticed tears on several cheeks. Even Great-aunt had dabbed at her eyes with a corner of her sari.

Later, lying in bed, Neela tried to recall the tune and remember the rest of the words, but she couldn't. She hummed a little bit of it, then gave up. She wished she could go and see the baoul. She was sure he'd be sitting on the porch of the ruined old Krishna temple on the other side of the pond, as always, humming a tune or just quietly thinking. He'd teach the song to her.

Tomorrow, she decided. *I'll go and ask him tomorrow.*

Bandits!

'Neela!' her cousin Rani scolded laughingly as she tucked the pleats of the orange silk sari into the top of Neela's petticoat. 'Can't you stand still, even for a couple of minutes?'

'But it's so exciting!' Neela said as she shifted from foot to foot. 'I want to go and see the lights, and how they've decorated the wedding area with flowers, and how Usha looks in her wedding clothes. And wait, isn't that the musician starting to play his shehnai? That must mean the bridegroom's party has arrived!'

'Well, unless you let me finish putting your sari on you,' Rani said, 'you aren't going to get to see anything! So you might as well stop fidgeting.'

Neela forced herself to stand quietly. Rani arranged the end of the sari so that it fell in neat pleats from Neela's shoulder down her back, using safety pins to secure it to Neela's silk taffeta blouse.

'That's so it won't slide off you, in case you forget and bend over suddenly!' Rani said, laughing. Then she stood back with a smile to admire the results.

'The cow girl has been transformed into a princess, if I say so myself!' she said, 'Here, take a look.'

Neela stared wide-eyed into the small hand mirror that Rani had given her. She wasn't used to seeing her reflection. The only mirror the family possessed was hung from a wall hook in her parents' room, and though Usha went in there several times a day to comb her hair, Neela never bothered to. *Is this really me, this pretty girl with sparkling black eyes lined with kajal, hair neatly braided down her back, and a small, round orange bindi in the middle of her forehead?* Neela wondered. *And the sari! Why, it's gorgeous! It makes me look at least fifteen!* Neela decided that it was worth being pinched and prodded for half an hour by Rani! Tomorrow she would be happy enough to get back to her frocks and skirts, to rescuing kites and splashing around with Budhi in the pond, but tonight she looked forward to sitting among the women and pretending that she was all grown up.

'Thank you for helping me,' Neela said in a proper, ladylike voice.

Rani grinned at Neela's formal tone as she pinned a white gardenia in her young cousin's hair. 'You sound just right, too! Why, before you know it, the women with grown sons will be fighting with each other to present a marriage offer to your mother!'

'Rani!'

'Just joking!' Rani said. 'Now, go see your mother. She has something to give you. And remember—take small, gliding steps—not like you're rushing to escape from a mad bull!'

Neela tried to follow Rani's instructions. It wasn't easy. Her feet kept getting caught in the pleats of the sari. *How do women manage to wear these things and still do all their housework?* Neela wondered. *At this rate, it'll take me all night just to walk down the corridor.*

Neela glanced around quickly and then lifted the sari to her knees. *There, that's better,* she thought as she ran to her mother's room. Outside the door she stopped and carefully smoothed down the pleats before her mother saw her.

Neela thought her mother looked lovely in a white silk sari with a red and gold border. 'Don't you look beautiful!' Ma said, giving Neela a kiss. 'And so grown-up! Why, you're already almost as tall as I am!' Neela gave a pleased smile. It wasn't too often that her mother was so approving of her. She vowed she'd be on her best behaviour the rest of the evening.

'And now, to complete your outfit, here are your earrings,' Sarada said, handing Neela the tiny golden hoops that she wore on special occasions. 'Here's your choker. And here are these, for your arms.' Neela fastened the choker, with its teardrop pendant, around her neck, then squeezed her hands through three sets of gold bangles that were getting a bit snug.

'Thank you, Ma,' she said, and turned to leave.

'Wait, wait!' Sarada said. She paused mysteriously, and then she handed Neela a small package wrapped in maroon velvet.

Neela opened it curiously, then drew in her breath in delighted surprise. It was a long gold chain, shining in the light of the lantern her mother held up. 'For me?' she breathed, not quite believing her eyes.

'Yes,' Sarada said. 'You're becoming a young woman, after all. Your father and I thought this would be a good occasion to give you some new jewellery. You'll be careful with it, won't you?'

Neela put on the gold chain and looked in the mirror. The chain glittered around her neck as though it held a kind of magic. It was beautiful, and she knew it must have cost her parents a lot of money.

'I'll be really careful,' she said, giving her mother a heartfelt hug, and appreciatively sniffing the scent of sandalwood soap that Sarada always used.

Neela sat among the women guests in the clearing by the side of the house, where the wedding was taking place. Lanterns were strung around the wedding area, and torches that were mounted on poles lighted up the crowd. But beyond the clearing, the thick grove of mango trees was dark as ink. Neela looked out thoughtfully on the mysterious darkness as she listened to the drawn-out notes of the shehnai. The notes were soft and sorrowful, yet full of joy at the same time. They celebrated the fact that her sister was starting a new life, but they mourned that Usha's girlhood was ending now that she was a bride. How many new responsibilities she would have as a wife!

Neela wondered what her sister was thinking. Usha sat next to her new husband in front of the wedding fire, repeating the words that the priest chanted. Neela thought that Usha looked beautiful in her red silk sari and all her gold wedding jewellery—a nose ring, a necklace, matching earrings, an armband, and bracelets—that their father had been saving for for years, because, as everyone knew, a daughter's wedding was an expensive affair. Neela could see that Usha was tired. Usha's fingers trembled as she offered handfuls of puffed rice into the fire. She didn't even glance at the gifts, which were piled up next to the wedding area. Fortunately, the wedding was almost over—the garlands of jasmine and chrysanthemums had been exchanged already. And the dowry—a bag of gold coins—had been handed by her father to Usha's father-in-law.

Thinking about the dowry upset Neela. Her parents had had to do without a lot of things to get all that money together. And still they had come up short. Finally, they had had to sell two of their cows. *It's unfair that the girl's parents should have to pay so much,* Neela thought once again. *After all, aren't Usha's in-laws gaining a new and valuable family member, someone to help them at home, for free, for the rest of her life?*

'I don't know where you get such ideas,' Sarada had said, displeased, when Neela had told her this earlier. 'Dowries for girls—that's the way it's always been.'

Neela's thoughts were interrupted by an uproar in the audience. People were standing up, pointing, and shouting something she couldn't make out. Women started screaming and running toward the house. Then she saw them, a group of men, their faces blackened with soot and oil to prevent easy recognition. They were brandishing weapons—mostly scythes and axes, and the leader carried a gun. *Where had they come from?* Neela wondered, strangely calm in spite of her fear. *And how was it that no one heard them until they were right in the middle of everything?*

The leader started to speak. His deep voice, full of authority, made the guests quiet down and listen.

'Brothers and Sisters! We don't intend to hurt anyone, as long as you do what we say—because we aren't ordinary robbers. We are swadeshis, freedom fighters. We've taken a vow not to rest until our motherland is liberated from the curse of the British, who treat Indians no better than dogs. But for that we need money. We need to train and feed our men. We need medical supplies for when they get wounded. And most of all, we need weapons. Do you know how much it costs to make a single bomb? Without proper weapons, how can we stand up against the might of the British army?

'So we ask for your help. We ask that every man in the wedding party give us what is in his pockets, and that each woman give us a piece of jewellery. In exchange, we'll give you liberty, and the right to walk with your head held high in your own country—or we will die in the process. It isn't too much to ask, is it?'

There was a murmuring in the crowd. Neela noticed the landowner, Ram Prasad Chowdhury, sitting in an armchair he'd had carried specially for him from his mansion. His arms were folded rigidly across his chest, and an annoyed look was on his face. It was clear that he wasn't eager to give the freedom fighters *anything*. The people around him glanced at him uncertainly—he was their leader, after all, and they wanted to do what he did.

Then a voice spoke up from a corner. 'No, it isn't! It isn't too much to ask. Good people—or should I call you goats and sheep—is a handful of money more important to you than a life of dignity? Or have you licked the boots of the British for so long that you've forgotten what a dignified life is?'

It was the baoul. He stood and held up a fist. 'Here's everything I have, all the coins that people gave me to listen to my songs. You can have it all. The Lord will provide for me again, I have no doubt of that.'

Some of the freedom fighters were coming through the crowd, holding out large pieces of cloth. The baoul dropped his coins onto one of these. They made a loud clinking as they fell. And, as though the sound released the guests from a spell, others began to reach into their pockets. Coins and notes began to fill up the cloths. Usha's father-in-law hesitated, then took out a gold piece from the dowry bag and dropped it on the cloth near him. Hari Charan—who didn't have anything else with him—gave his gold ring. Neela couldn't see what the landowner did—there were too many people milling about in front of him. Women were taking off jewellery—mostly small items, Neela noted. But at least they were giving! Usha whispered something to her new husband, and he nodded. She slipped off one of her bracelets and laid it on the cloth. The baoul was singing *Vande Mataram* in an ecstatic voice, and the freedom fighters, who were obviously familiar with the song, joined in.

Then someone was in front of Neela, holding out a cloth. The cloth was orange, green and white, and a turban of the same color was tied around the man's head. *But no,* Neela thought, *he's really a boy.* In spite of his blackened face, Neela could see that he was only about sixteen or so. Neela was surprised. *He must have left his home and taken up the scary business of fighting the British! What gave him the strength to do that? And his mother—does she weep for him at night, wondering where he is?*

Neela was about to take off her earrings, but then she changed her mind. She unclasped her new gold chain and put it down carefully on the cloth. It sparkled brilliantly among all the other items, clearly the most valuable piece in there. She felt a moment of regret, but she was happy, too. She knew she'd get into a lot of trouble when her mother found out—but surely her father would understand!

A grin split open the boy's face. 'Hey! Thanks!' he said. 'That will be a lot of help!' His smile was very white against his dark face, and there was a slight gap between the front teeth. She liked the openness of his smile and its honesty. She wanted to ask him so many things about the freedom fighters, but there wasn't time. The leader was hurrying his men, telling them it was time they were gone.

Hari Charan stood up. 'Won't you stay and share the wedding feast with us?' he asked.

The leader laughed. 'It's a tempting offer! The food certainly smells good! But, no—it's best we move on. One never knows if there are British informants in a gathering.'

Did Neela imagine it, or did he look, for a moment, directly at the landowner?

'Neela!' called her father. 'Run to the cook and ask him to pack a bundle of sweets for the freedom fighters. Hurry!'

'It'll only take a minute,' he told the leader.

'I won't say no to that—my boys haven't had anything good to eat in weeks. Many days, it's dangerous even to light a fire.'

Neela picked up the hem of her sari—she didn't care what people thought—and ran to the cook. He had heard what Hari Charan had said and was ready with a big earthenware pot, which he handed to Neela. She hurried back with it and breathlessly handed the pot to the boy she'd given her gold chain to.

'Thanks again!' he said as she smiled. 'We'll think of you when we eat tonight!'

The leader spoke once more to the wedding guests. 'Good people,' he said, 'help our struggle by not buying British goods. Wear only handloom cotton that's woven by your own countrymen. Ladies, throw away all the glass bangles you have—they've been imported. Let's hurt the British in their pocketbooks, too!' Then he took off his turban and handed it to Hari Charan. 'Here's something for you. Keep it carefully. These are the colours of our flag, the flag of a new India. I hope you'll be able to fly it soon! Let's go, men! Good wishes to the bride and groom! May your children be born into an independent land!' At the edge of the clearing, he paused and turned once more. 'You're a good man, Hari Charan,' he said. 'You should join us. The motherland needs men like you.'

'I don't believe in violence,' Neela's father said. 'Killing people is not right, not even for independence.'

'Do you think I like it?' the leader said, his voice hard. 'All these men—and boys—who've trusted me and left everything—home, safety, their loved ones, do you think I like putting their lives in danger? But what other way is there? You don't think the British are just going to hand over the country with a handshake, do you? Have you forgotten Jallianwala Bagh, where they massacred thousands of our innocent, unarmed people, including women and children? No, the British must be forced to quit India—and I'll use whatever means I must to achieve that.' Then he melted into the darkness.

Everyone at the wedding feast was talking excitedly about the bandits. There were many different opinions.

'Rascals, every last one of them!' the landowner said loudly, his mouth full of goat curry. 'Who knows what they'll do with the money they've collected. Probably use it for themselves! Hari Charan, you're too gullible. You should throw away that tricoloured cloth quickly, before you get into trouble. And why did you have to go and give them the wedding sweets? They don't deserve such a courtesy.'

'Somehow I don't think they're liars, Ram Prasad Chowdhury,' Hari Charan said, respectfully but firmly. Neela noticed that he touched the cloth, which he'd hung around his neck, with careful fingers as he spoke.

'Even so, what they're doing is no good, blowing up railroads and telegraph poles. They've even tried to assassinate some of the British high officials. What'll happen to the country if the British are gone? Looting and anarchy, that's all I see ahead of us if they win!' the landowner said heatedly.

'It's a good thing that Mother India has a few sons, at least, who care more about her than about their pockets,' the baoul said dryly.

'You! You're nothing but trouble, too!' shouted the landowner. 'For all I know, you're hand in hand with those bandits. Singing forbidden songs, inciting people to foolishness! I want you out of this village by tomorrow morning. I'm going to instruct my watchmen to give you a good beating if they see you around after that.'

Hari Charan started to protest, but the baoul stopped him. He gave an ironic bow to the landowner. 'Your wish is my command,' he said. 'Besides, I've finished what I came here to do. I have work elsewhere now.' He picked up his ektara and staff and started to walk away.

Neela pushed past the wedding guests to follow him, but the end of her sari kept getting caught on things. The baoul was already at the edge of the clearing by the time she caught up with him. 'You can't leave like this, Baoul dadu!' she panted. 'Why, it's night-time! It isn't safe out there, in the woods and fields.'

He smiled at her. 'Little Granddaughter,' he said. 'Is it any safer in the villages and towns? Sometimes men are more dangerous than wild beasts. But don't worry—I have my staff in my hand and faith in my heart. I'll be fine.'

'But I wanted to learn that song from you—*Vande*—'

'*Vande Mataram!* Just remember those two words, and say them to yourself. I'll teach the rest to you next time. Meanwhile, think of Mother India and what you can do for her. If nothing else, pray for the freedom fighters.'

'I will! But you haven't eaten anything—'

'Next time,' smiled the baoul. He laid his calloused palm gently on her head. Then he, too, melted into the darkness of the grove.

Good-byes

The day after the wedding was not a good one for Neela.

The trouble really began the night before, after the feast. The excitement from the coming of the freedom fighters had finally died down, and people began to leave for home, commenting loudly on what a fine wedding celebration it had been. The food was excellent, they said. The *luchis* were crisp and golden-brown, the fish was fresh, and the spices in the goat curry were just right. And the desserts—sweet pink yogurt and sandesh, delicately flavoured with rosewater—melted in your mouth! It was clear that people in the village would be talking about the meal for a long time.

'The bride and groom looked so good together,' a neighbour had said as she was leaving. 'That Usha is so pretty. And did you see how she kept her eyes modestly lowered all through the ceremony, as a good girl should!'

'The other daughter, Neela, looked pretty too, in her new sari,' responded someone else. 'She's growing up to be a smart girl. Did you see how she ran to get the sweets for the freedom fighters? She wasn't scared of their gun and knives, that one.'

'But it's hard to imagine her sitting quietly like her sister—even at her own wedding!' said the neighbour. 'Whoever gets her as a daughter-in-law will have trouble controlling her!'

Neela, who overheard this conversation, felt her face grow hot with anger. *Why does everyone feel they have to control girls—even after they're married? Why are women expected to sit quietly and silently, embroidering and making pickles, while men get to make all the important decisions and go to all the exciting places? Why can't a girl be a freedom fighter?*

She pictured herself as a freedom fighter, complete with blackened face and turban, in arm-to-arm combat with a British soldier. The soldier's face was pink and sweaty, and he lunged at her with a sword. But she evaded him easily, and with a sharp twist of her own sword, sent his sword flying across the—

'Neela!' Sarada's voice broke into her fantasy. 'It's late. You need to go to bed right away. I need you to help me early in the morning with setting up things for the good-bye ceremony. Go take off your sari and put on your frock. Fold the sari neatly and bring it to me so I can put it away. Oh, yes, bring me your jewellery, also.'

Neela did as she was told. Her heart pounded loudly as she wrapped the earrings, choker and bangles in the velvet cloth that had held the gold chain. She handed Sarada the sari and the small velvet bundle, hoping she would lock them away. But Sarada stopped to check.

'Let me see—ah, just as I thought. You've forgotten the chain in your room. Go get it, Neela.'

Neela didn't move.

'What's the matter? I'll let you have it again tomorrow, if you want. It's just safer to lock it up at night. It's very expensive, you know.'

With a dry throat, Neela told Sarada what she had done. She expected her mother to shout at her, maybe even to slap her. But Sarada only stared at her. The look of horrified disbelief on her face was worse than any slap.

'How could you do that, Neela?' she said in a broken voice. 'It was to be part of your dowry. How will we ever afford another chain like that? It's good to think of your motherland, and all those fancy notions, but what about your *family*? Shouldn't you be thinking of us, too? Do you know how long it took your father to save for that chain?'

Neela bent her head, feeling terribly guilty about the pain and worry she had caused her mother. But what she had done wasn't wrong, she knew it in her bones. Oh, here was another of those complicated times when duties clashed with each other! She wished her father were here. He wouldn't be so angry about what she had done, she just knew it!

'Go to bed,' Sarada was saying sternly. 'Tomorrow, after Usha leaves, your father and I will have to decide what your punishment is going to be.'

The morning was a busy one, for which Neela was grateful. She had to set out breakfast for the bride and groom and then help load all their gifts into the bullock carts that would carry them to Usha's new home. But through it all, she was aware of her mother's displeasure. Sarada spoke to her only once, to instruct her about what she should do, and even then she did not look at Neela but only at a spot on the wall behind her.

One whole bullock cart was taken up with just the gifts that her parents had got for Gopal, Usha's husband. This, too, was part of the dowry. Once the wedding plans had been finalized, Gopal's father had given Hari Charan a detailed list, including the names of the stores from which each item should be bought.

Neela knew that the gifts included traditional Indian clothes in both silk and cotton—dhotis and kurtas—as well as English shirts and pants from the Sialdah Bazaar. There was also a gold pocket watch in a decorated case, with Gopal's initials engraved on it. There were many household items—bedsheets, quilts, and pillowcases that Usha had painstakingly embroidered with a peacock design, steel pots and pans, and a whole stack of large, shiny brass plates. There was more, but Neela's eyes were caught by the shoes.

The shoes were made of black leather and very shiny, with crisp, thin shoelaces to match. Neela picked one up, fascinated. She hadn't seen many shoes—most people in the village went barefoot. Her father did have a pair of sandals that he wore when he went to Calcutta, but they were old and worn. She ran her hand appreciatively around the soft inner edge. There was an embossed sign there. With difficulty—because she had studied only a little English—Neela deciphered the words. They read, 'Made in Great Britain'.

Neela put the shoe down quickly. Before yesterday, she wouldn't have given the matter a thought, but now she felt that somehow, by buying those foreign-made shoes, her family had betrayed the freedom fighters. And yet— what could they have done? Not to buy what Usha's in-laws had specified would have caused trouble for Usha in her new home.

Everyone wept when Usha left: Sarada, the neighbouring women who had come to see her off, and Usha herself, who had been too distraught to eat any breakfast. Even Neela, who rarely cried, felt her eyes filling with tears as she wondered how things would be for her sister now. Would her mother-in-law (whom Usha was supposed to call Ma from this day) scold Usha if she failed to wake up early, as she so often did at home? Would she criticize Usha's cooking and sewing? Would she make her do all the hardest chores around the house? Neela had heard lots of horror stories about mothers-in-law. She said a quick prayer for her sister as she waved at Usha, swathed in a veil that made her look like a stranger, gazing mournfully at the home that was no longer hers.

Why does a bride have to go to her husband's home after getting married? Neela thought rebelliously. *Why does she have to make all the changes?*

Neela took one last look at her sister as the cart disappeared around the bend in the road.

Perhaps I won't get married at all, Neela said to herself.

At that moment, her father called to her. 'Neela! Your mother and I need to talk to you.'

It was the summons Neela had been dreading. It was bad enough to have upset her mother. How would she bear it if her father, whom she loved most of all, was also angry with her?

With trembling footsteps, she followed her parents to their room.

Hari Charan did not waste time in small talk.

'Neela,' he said, his voice serious, 'your mother told me what you did. You know that gold chain was very valuable. Why did you give it away like that?'

Neela swallowed. Her lips were dry and her heart was hammering against her ribs. A frown drew her father's eyebrows together as he stared at her, making him look very stern. Sarada sat beside him on their bed, looking even sterner.

Neela wanted to throw herself into her father's arms, the way she did when she was a little girl. But she knew it wouldn't work. She wasn't little anymore, and she had to take responsibility for her actions.

'I'm very sorry that I've upset you both so much, Baba. I didn't realize the gold chain was for my dowry—Ma gave it to me, so I thought it was mine. And I don't think it was wrong of me to give something so valuable to the freedom fighters—'

'See!' said Sarada angrily. 'You see how stubborn she is!'

Neela took a deep breath and continued. 'After all, they're risking their lives for our sake, to make us independent. Didn't you say so yourself? Didn't you tell me you admired them, too?' She stopped for a moment, then squared her shoulders. 'But I'm willing to accept any punishment you give me.'

Her father was silent for a long moment. He looked preoccupied, as though he was thinking of something other than Neela's problem. But then Sarada nudged him and he came back to the present with a start.

'Yes, I do have a punishment for you.'

Neela looked at him nervously. 'Are you going to beat me?'

'No, I'm not! I don't believe that teaches anyone anything.'

'Please don't make me stop my lessons, Baba—they mean so much to me—'

'Of course I won't. What good will that do? Instead, I'm going to give you a chance to earn back the money you gave away. Our maid Ganga told me she doesn't want to work anymore—she's getting too old. I want you to take over her job in the barn. You're to do everything—feed and bathe the cows, clean the stalls, cut up the hay for them, and milk them. Because of Budhi, you already know how to do most of this. Your mother will put aside the money we save this way each month, until we have enough to buy another gold chain.'

'I will, I will!' Neela said earnestly, feeling very lucky. He was a fair and intelligent man, her father! Other fathers would have caned their children, at the very least. But he had given her the chance to do something positive to make up for what she'd done, and to help the household at the same time.

'Let me warn you that it'll take a long time—a couple of years, at least,' he said.

'I don't mind,' Neela said. 'I'll take really good care of the cows. And I'll try not to do anything else to upset you and Ma.' She looked at Sarada pleadingly. Sarada didn't smile back, but she gave a little nod.

'Good!' Hari Charan said. 'Now let's go to the barn and see what needs to be done.'

Once they had entered the barn, though, her father wasn't interested in looking around. Instead, he sat on a bale of hay and motioned to Neela to join him. He didn't talk but stared into a dark corner where rusty old plows were stored. In the dim light of the barn, his face looked worried.

'Baba,' said Neela, taking his left hand in hers. She loved her father's hands, large and calloused, but so gentle at the same time. She stroked a V-shaped scar on the back of his hand, left there from a childhood accident with a scythe. 'Is something wrong? Is it what I did?'

'No, my daughter. It isn't that at all. It's just that I've made a decision, and I'm trying to find words to tell you about it.'

Neela's heart sped up. What could it be? It was nothing

she would like, she could guess that from his face. Surely he wasn't trying to arrange a marriage for her already! But his answer, when it came, was so unexpected that it left her wordless.

'I'm going to Calcutta,' he said. 'I'm leaving tomorrow after lunch. There's a train that stops at Shona Gram in the late afternoon, and I want to catch that.'

'But, but—' Neela stammered, distressed, 'why do you need to go to Calcutta again? You just went there a month ago to do all the wedding shopping.'

Her father shook his head. 'This time it's not for myself, or for family matters. I want to go and see what our leaders are doing.'

'Which leaders?'

'There's a group there called the Congress Party. They've been asking the British to hand over the governing of the country to them for a long time. One of their top members, Mahatma Gandhi, has called for a general boycott next week, not just of British-made things but also of their courts, offices, railways—everything. There's going to be a big march—a peaceful march, the old baoul told me, because Gandhi doesn't believe in violence. Daughter, I want to find out more about it, maybe even take part in it! I've sat in the safety of my house for too long.'

'But, Baba—' Neela's throat was so dry she could barely get the words out, 'won't it be dangerous?'

'Yes, the baoul warned me of it. Even though our people are acting peacefully, the army and police, which are controlled by the British, are not. They've killed or wounded a lot of people and have thrown even more into prison. But Neela—I can't forget what that freedom fighter said. India needs me at this critical time. I'll never forgive myself if I don't go.' He paused and made himself smile reassuringly. 'Don't look so worried—I plan to come back right after the march to support the boycott, in a week or so. After all, I must prepare the fields for next season's planting.'

'Have you told Ma?'

Her father looked a little uncomfortable. 'Well, not really . . . not quite,' he admitted. 'You know how upset your mother gets. And right now, with Usha gone—well, I didn't think it would be a good idea. I told her that I'm going to Calcutta to buy some high-quality seed for our crops. It's not exactly a lie. I plan to do that as well.'

Then he put his hand on Neela's shoulder. 'But I told you because I feel I can trust you to help your mother, take care of things, and keep my secret.'

'I promise!' Neela nodded emphatically, her chest swelling with pride. 'I won't let you down!'

'There's one more thing,' her father said, his eyes somber. 'If for some reason I'm unable to come back—'

'No!' Neela cried, clapping her hand over his mouth. But he moved it away and completed his sentence '—then you must tell your mother the truth, so that she knows I died for our country.'

Neela bit her lip to keep in the tears as she watched Hari Charan walk down the dirt path that led away from their house. In his clean but worn dhoti and kurta, with a bag slung over his shoulder, he looked so—defenseless. The thought surprised her. She had always looked up to her father as the strong one, the one who could solve all her problems. But now she noticed how thin his hair was getting, how it was sprinkled with gray. How would he ever be able to stand up against the might of the British empire?

'Don't be sad, now,' Sarada said, giving her an unexpected hug. 'He'll just be gone for a few days. With all your new chores, the time will pass before you realize it. And you know he always brings us a surprise gift when he comes back! That'll be something for you to look forward to!'

Neela nodded wordlessly. What her father had told her in the barn hung inside her chest, solid as a stone. At that time, she had been so proud to be his confidante— but now she wished he had told Sarada, too. Then they could have worried together. Together, they could have prayed for his safety.

She watched her father's figure, small with distance, disappear around a bend in the road, feeling lonelier than she ever had in her life.

The Secret Guest

Neela emptied a heaped basket of cut-up hay into Budhi's feeding tray. She mixed some fresh grass and leaves into it, along with some grain and a handful of the roots that Panditji, her teacher, had given her to keep the cattle healthy. Panditji, who also served as the village apothecary and vet, had been very helpful to Neela and her mother during Hari Charan's absence. He often stopped after lessons to take a look at the cattle, and he never charged them extra for it.

Budhi, who was hungry, mooed loudly and pushed against Neela, trying to get at her food.

'Oh, Budhi!' Neela said. 'Your life is so simple! As long as I give you enough to eat, tether you under the mango trees so you can chew your cud in peace, and take you down to the pond for your bath, you're happy. I wish I could be like you!' She laid her head on the cow's flank and added, in a whisper, 'I'm so worried about Baba. It's already been a week since he left, and we've heard nothing. Ma thinks I'm silly to worry. She thinks he's been delayed because so many rail lines have been destroyed recently by freedom fighters. She could be right—but I just have a bad feeling about it. And you're the only one I can tell.' Neela stood up straight, shaking her head. 'Well, I'd better stop mooning around and fetch more feed. Soon the farmhands will bring the buffaloes back from tilling the fields—and they'll be hungry.'

She'd almost reached the door of the barn when she heard a hollow cough behind her. Surprised, she spun around. 'Budhi? Did you make that awful sound? Are you all right?'

But Budhi was chewing contentedly.

Neela heard the coughing sound again. It seemed to come from behind the stacks of hay. Could a wild animal—a mongoose or fox—have gotten into the barn at night? But how could that be? She was always careful to latch the door after she milked the cows in the evening. There was the sound once more, followed by a wheezing this time. Her heart beating fast, Neela picked up a stout piece of bamboo and tiptoed over to the stacks. Between the stacks and the wall there was a small, hollowed-out space. Surely it hadn't been there before! Cautiously, she poked her stick in the space, ready to run if necessary. But instead of an animal's snarl, she heard a distinctly human, distinctly male voice.

'Ow!' it said.

It was a thief! 'Stay right where you are,' Neela shouted. 'Don't move, or—' she looked around desperately, '—or I'll chop you to pieces with the hay cutter!' If only she could keep the man in there until the farmhands came! They would give him such a beating that he wouldn't dare to even think of coming back.

'I'm not planning to move,' said the voice, sounding a bit amused. But then it coughed again. 'In fact, I can't move too well.' It sounded kind of weak—but maybe that was just a trick. Neela glanced at the door of the barn. Where were those farmhands? Probably sitting in the shade of some tree, smoking. Maybe they would hear her if she screamed really loudly. She opened her mouth to give it a try.

'Neela,' said the voice, 'I need your help.'

'How do you know my name?' she asked, startled.

'I heard your father say it the day of the wedding.'

'Who *are* you? And if you're not a thief, why are you here?'

'I'm the person who was collecting valuables for the freedom fighters. You gave me your gold chain, remember? I got hurt in an encounter with the police— and I'm too hurt to travel far. I can't go to a hospital— they'd throw me in jail, or worse. So I came here. Your father seemed like a man of honour—I didn't think he would turn me in. I was hoping he would let me stay here until I got better—'

Neela heard a commotion at the door. The farmhands were returning with the buffaloes! Quickly, she covered up the opening with some loose straw and hurried to the door.

'I'll take care of the buffaloes,' she told the men. 'You can go on home.'

The men went off happily as Neela brought in the buffaloes. Then she closed the barn door, wishing it had a latch on the inside, and hurried back to the injured boy. 'Can you come out from behind there?' she asked.

He crawled out slowly. She drew in a breath at how ill he looked. The soot had worn off parts of his face, and his skin was pale. The left side of his kurta was red with blood, and when she lifted it, she could see a dirty, makeshift bandage of rags tied around his shoulder. She touched the bandage to see if the wound was still bleeding. It was dry and crusty—but even that slight pressure made him groan and shut his eyes in pain. When she touched his forehead, it was hot with fever.

Neela's mind raced. What should she do? She didn't have the skill to nurse him. But whom could she trust? Her mother didn't have much sympathy for the freedom fighters, especially since Neela had given away her chain. Besides, she'd be unwilling to harbour someone the police were looking for. Neela couldn't blame her. If the police found the boy in their home, Neela's family was sure to be punished severely. Oh, how she wished her father were here, so she could hand the problem over to him!

'Can you get me some water?' the boy asked faintly.

Neela jumped to her feet, ashamed that she hadn't thought of it. 'Of course!' she said, and rushed out the door to the pump, where she filled a bucket. Next, she peeked into the kitchen. Luckily, it was empty, so she took a glass and a couple of wheat rutis that the cook had roasted. Finally, she went to her room and rummaged through her clothes until she found an old shift.

Back in the barn, she gave the boy some water, holding his head steady so he could drink. 'Not so fast,' she cautioned him as he gulped the water down thirstily. She remembered that her mother always said that to her when she had a fever. She washed the boy's face, and finally, with fingers that trembled, she undid the bandage.

The wound looked terrible, with its torn and swollen flesh. Blood had dried in dirty, crusted patches around it, and seeing it made Neela dizzy. But she knew she couldn't afford to be weak right now. So she took a deep breath, tore a strip off her shift, wet it, and tried to clean the wound as best she could. It must have hurt a lot—the boy stiffened his whole body and bit his lip to stop himself from crying out. She wasn't sure if there was something still in the wound—a bullet, perhaps—and she was afraid to ask. When it looked a little better, she bandaged it up and broke the rutis into small pieces for the boy. He ate a few mouthfuls, but then shook his head.

'I'm too tired,' he said. 'Just let me rest.' When Neela touched his forehead, it felt hotter than before, and this scared her.

What should I do? What should I do? The thought spun around inside her head as she rearranged the bales of hay loosely around the boy, hiding him again. She fed the buffaloes so that their hungry cries would not attract her mother to the barn. *Maybe I could look in the medicine chest for the pills Panditji gave me last year, when I caught the malaria fever?* she thought. But the chest was kept in her parents' room, and Sarada was sure to ask questions if she caught Neela looking in there. Should she pretend she was sick herself, with a terrible headache? She knew that headache medicine often reduced fever as well. But then Sarada would make her stay in bed, and she wouldn't be able to come to the barn.

Baba! Neela thought, closing her eyes. *Help me!* She tried to call up her father's face—perhaps it would give her a hint of what to do. But instead, she saw another face etched against her squeezed-shut eyelids. Panditji's!

She would have to trust her teacher. There was no one else.

'Panditji! Panditji!' Neela called.

Panditji, who had been resting in the cool darkness of his room after his midday meal, came out rubbing his eyes.

'Neela!' he said in surprise. 'What are you doing here? Look at you—you're drenched with sweat. Did you run all the way here?'

Neela nodded, still out of breath. Panditji poured her a glass of cold water from the earthenware pitcher in his room, and handed her a palm-leaf fan to fan herself. 'Sit down for a minute and relax. Then you can tell me what's wrong.'

But Neela couldn't wait. 'Can you keep a secret, Panditji? Please.'

'Depends on what it is,' he said, looking at her with a frown. 'If it's something serious, your mother will need to know.'

'It's a boy—he's badly hurt—'

'Who is it? One of the farmhands' children?'

'No.' Neela looked pleadingly at her teacher. 'He's a—'

she lowered her voice, '—a freedom fighter.'

Panditji's face grew anxious. 'Oh no! How did you get mixed up with that bunch of troublemakers?'

'Please come with me,' Neela tugged at his hand. 'He's really sick. I'll tell you everything on the way.'

'If the police come looking for him, we'll all end up in jail!' he said. Then he gave a resigned sigh. 'But I guess I can't just let him die, even if he is a freedom fighter. One thing's definite—and don't try to change my mind, young lady—your mother will have to be told about this.'

The pandit washed the wound with warm water and examined it carefully to make sure nothing was lodged inside.

'You're lucky, young man,' he declared as he put some ointment on the wound and bandaged it up again. 'If there was a bullet in there, you'd have to have an operation, and that's quite beyond my skills. Looks as if the bullet glanced off you. You've lost a fair amount of blood, but the wound's not deep.'

The boy tried to speak, but the pandit held up his hand. 'Don't tell me what happened. I don't want to know!'

Panditji gave the boy a couple of fever pills to chew and set the bottle of pills within easy reach for him to take again at night.

'Drink lots of water, and eat some rutis if you're up to it. Once the fever goes down, you can have a little rice and some fish soup. I'll tell Neela's mother.'

Neela's breath caught in her throat. So he really was going to tell Sarada!

'Don't look so scared! Young lady, you don't know your mother if you really think she'd throw a sick boy out on the street,' Panditji said with a wry smile. He turned to the boy. 'I'll come back tomorrow to make sure there's no infection. After that, Neela should be able to take care of you. The most important thing is to rest and get proper nutrition.'

'Thank you,' said the boy in a faint voice.

'The best thanks you can give me is to get better quickly and leave before we all get into trouble,' the pandit replied.

Neela carried the milking pail carefully to the barn. Inside the pail was hidden a large covered bowl of rice and dal, and another one of fish curry. After Samar—that was the boy's name—ate, she would wash the dishes in the pond when no one was around and would sneak them back to the kitchen.

'I don't want *anyone* to know about that boy,' Sarada had said emphatically, after she reluctantly agreed to the pandit's request that she let the young freedom fighter stay in their barn until he healed. 'And I don't want to see him myself. That way, if the police ever question me, I can truthfully say I never set eyes on such a person.' She'd turned to Neela sternly. 'I don't want you to spend too much time with him, either. You've got enough rebellious ideas in your head already. Just check his wound, give him his food, finish your regular jobs in the barn, and come straight back to your room, do you hear?'

Neela had agreed willingly. She was very thankful that her mother was letting Samar stay.

During the first few days, Samar was too weak to say much. However, after he recovered a little, he started talking to Neela as she did her chores in the barn. After a few more days, he helped her with some of them. Perhaps he was just lonely—and bored, too, because he wasn't used to lying around doing nothing. Or could it be that he liked her? A little shiver went through Neela when she thought this.

Samar told her about his group of freedom fighters. There were about twenty of them. Their leader's name was Biren. That was the man who had spoken to them at Usha's wedding.

'A kinder, braver man I've never known,' said Samar. 'Biren was a schoolteacher in Calcutta before he became a swadeshi. But one day someone introduced him to Netaji Subhash Bose—'

'Who is Netaji Subhash Bose?' Neela asked, feeling ignorant. But she knew Samar wouldn't mind explaining.

'He's one of our greatest leaders! Comes from a very rich Calcutta family. Went to London for his studies, even. He could have had a great career in the civil service, but he declared he'd never be a slave to England. He has pledged his life to serve his country—to do whatever is necessary to rid India of these foreign vermin. He's afraid of nothing!'

Neela's eyes were bright with wonder. 'He sounds like

one of the heroes out of an old tale like the *Ramayana*!'

'He is! Biren has sworn to follow him to the death—and so have I!'

There was such conviction in Samar's voice that it made the hairs stand up on Neela's arm. 'But you're so young! How did you become a freedom fighter?'

'I ran away from home!' He grinned at the shocked look on her face.

'But your parents—?'

'I don't have parents—they died when I was little. I was living with my uncle and going to school in Calcutta—the same school where Biren taught. I hated living in my uncle's house. He's very rich, and he always made me remember that I was the poor relation. Also, he's a judge at the big courthouse in Calcutta, and very pro-British. Why, he even has pictures of the viceroy and His Majesty hanging on his living room wall! It was sickening! I was dying to get away from that house.'

'But wasn't there anyone there who cared for you?' Neela asked, feeling sad for the orphaned Samar.

'Actually, there is someone. My cousin, Bimala. She's like an older sister to me. You see, her mother died when she was young, too. So she knew what it meant to be lonely and unhappy. I still keep in touch with her from time to time, because she'd worry so much otherwise.'

'What did you have to do to become a freedom fighter?' Neela asked.

'We had to train for it. We were made to walk from one end of the city to the other in the height of summer with no shoes,' Samar said. 'Do you know, it gets so hot that the pitch melts and sticks to the soles of your feet, burning them? And in the monsoon season, we went without umbrellas and remained in wet clothes all day to make us strong. We exercised for hours. Practised wrestling and martial arts with staffs.'

Neela stared at him in admiration. 'Really!'

'And that's not all!' Samar couldn't help giving her a proud smile. 'We had to go without food for days on end. We were sent into the countryside with no money and had to live off the land. We've been taught how to disguise ourselves to pass as peasants, old people, and even women! And, most importantly, we were taught to make bombs and use them. Guns also—though we have too little money for each of us to have one.'

'Have you ever fired a gun?' Neela asked in fascinated horror. 'Have you ever . . . shot anyone?'

'I've practiced with a gun. I'm not sure how I'd feel if I had to shoot someone.' Samar took a deep breath. 'I hope it never comes to that. But if he's a traitor to our motherland, or one of her enemies, I'd do it! How else will India become independent?'

'My father's gone to Calcutta to help with the independence movement, too,' Neela found herself saying, although she hadn't planned to. 'I'm worried, because we haven't heard from him in quite a while.'

Samar looked concerned. 'There's been a lot of trouble in Calcutta lately.' He gave her hand a squeeze. 'But try not to worry until you know for sure that there's something to worry about. That's something else we've learned as freedom fighters.'

All that evening, Neela felt comforted as she remembered his words—and the firm grip of his hand. *I won't worry,* she told herself. *Not until I'm sure there's something to worry about.*

Bang! Bang! Bang! Neela sprang up in bed, still half-asleep. Were those gunshots she was hearing? No, someone was banging on their front door. Who would come here at this time of night—it must be two or three a.m.—and make so much noise? It sounded like they were about to break down the door.

She heard her mother's frightened voice calling for their manservant.

'Rasik, get the lantern and come with me.'

Neela, too, followed them, her heart tight with fear.

Sarada opened the door. There were four or five constables in khaki uniforms outside. They were carrying rifles.

'What do you mean by disturbing innocent householders like this?' Sarada asked indignantly. But underneath, Neela could see that she was scared.

The constables didn't bother answering her. They pushed her aside and stepped into the house.

'Wait!' Sarada shouted. 'Stop! How dare you come into our house like this!'

'Don't try to stop us from doing the government's work, lady!' said their leader roughly. 'We've received information that you're harbouring a terrorist. We're going to search the house right now.'

'Go ahead!' Sarada said. Neela could see that she was trying to act as though she didn't care, but there was a quiver in her voice. Neela looked around to see if there was any way she could go and warn Samar.

But the head constable pointed at them. 'Sit right here, and don't move! One of my men will be watching you. And let me tell you—if we find that terrorist here, things will go badly with you.'

'And when you don't?' Sarada asked. Neela was amazed that she dared to talk back to the constable. Truly, as Panditji had said, she had underestimated her mother. 'Then you'll owe us a big apology for disturbing our sleep and for scaring my daughter half to death!'

Neela started to protest. Then she realized what Sarada was doing. *She's trying to delay them from starting the search.* In spite of her fear, Neela felt pride for her clever and brave mother.

It didn't work. The constables didn't even bother to answer Sarada. They were already crashing through the house, checking under the beds, knocking over furniture, throwing down pots and pans and creating a great clamor. One of them even ran his bayonet through a large sack of rice, spilling the grains onto the floor.

'No one's here, saab,' one of the men called.

'As I could have told you before you created all that mess,' Sarada said coldly. 'Do you know how long it'll take us to clean all this up?'

The head constable didn't look so confident anymore. 'Are there any other buildings nearby?'

'There's the outhouse,' Neela spoke up. 'You're welcome to look there—though I must warn you, it doesn't smell too good!'

A constable was sent to look, but he came back and reported that no one was there.

The head constable went outside and shone his flashlight around. 'What's that big, low building to the side?' he asked.

'That's just the barn,' Neela said. She spoke casually, but she was worried that they'd search it—and maybe find Samar.

'Men! Go take a look!' he barked.

'Wait, you'll disturb all the cattle!' Neela cried. 'Let me go first and settle them.' She started toward the barn, but the constable grabbed her arm.

'Oh, no, you don't!' he said.

Neela's throat was dry, but she made herself speak. 'Don't blame me, then, if the cows break their tethers and come after you. We have some big buffaloes in there, too.'

The constables looked at each other.

'We can't shoot at them, either,' said one man. The others nodded. They all knew how sacred cattle were. Kill a cow, the Hindu scriptures clearly declared, and you'd go straight to hell.

'Oh, very well,' said their leader. 'Come with us.'

Neela tried to make as much noise as she could as she walked with the men. But was it enough to warn Samar? She wasn't sure.

As soon as they reached the barn, the constables flung open the door and rushed in. The frightened cattle started mooing loudly. The buffaloes stomped and snorted. Neela tried to calm them as best she could. Then she hugged Budhi, pressing her face into the cow's neck. 'Please, God, please, God,' she prayed under her breath.

'Doesn't look like anyone's been here in a long time, saab,' she heard a man say.

It was almost dawn by the time the constables left, grumbling and complaining.

'Wait till I catch that informer!' the leader spat as he left. 'Making us leave our warm beds, and all for nothing!'

Neela stayed at the barn, her arms around Budhi's neck. She was too weak with relief to move. Samar had heard them, then, and had managed to escape—probably through one of the windows. And he'd removed all traces of his stay here so that Neela and her mother would not be found out. Her heart filled with thankfulness, and then with worry. He wasn't fully healed yet. Was he safe? Would he be all right?

'Oh, Budhi!' she said sadly. 'I don't even know how to get in touch with him. I'll probably never see him again.'

Out of habit, she reached under the rope tied around Budhi's neck to scratch the soft skin beneath her cow's throat. Something crackled against her hand.

There was a scrap of paper wrapped tightly around the rope.

In the early morning light, Neela read:

I can't thank you enough. If you ever need help, go to Bimala, at 99 Milford Lane, near Park Street. She'll know how to reach me.

'Budhi! Budhi!' Neela cried in joy, hugging the cow so tightly that she mooed in protest. 'To think that he made time to write this for me, even though his life was in danger!' She memorized the address and then tore the paper into tiny pieces and mixed them in with Budhi's feed.

'Sorry!' she said to her cow. 'But each one of us has to do our bit for the motherland!'

Bad News

Carrying a wicker basket of freshly picked marigolds from their courtyard, Neela walked behind her mother along the dirt path that led to the temple of Goddess Kali. Neela was wearing a new sky-blue sari with peacocks woven into it, and silver anklets on her feet. Sarada carried a covered brass bowl that was filled with sweets she had made that morning to offer to the goddess, for they were going to do a special puja, a prayer ceremony, for Hari Charan's welfare. It had been almost three weeks since he had left for Calcutta, and they had received no word of him.

'I don't know what's wrong,' Sarada had said in a worried voice. 'But I hope that if we do the puja, the goddess will bless us and send him back to us safely—and soon.'

Neela was worried, too. She wondered if she should tell her mother why Baba had gone to Calcutta.

Ma's face was thinner, and there were dark circles under her eyes. Neela suspected that she wasn't sleeping too well. Neela wasn't sleeping well herself. Even when she worked extra hard at her chores, hoping to tire herself out, her dreams were filled with garbled, disturbing images: the face of the mysterious and beautiful woman, with the sad eyes and the crown of jewels; Samar, smiling as a great fire blazed behind him, saying something she couldn't hear; her father, looking gaunt and ill, sitting in the shadow of a great, black wall.

'Walk faster, my dear,' Sarada said. 'The temple bells are ringing already.'

Neela lifted up her sari a little, to walk more easily. She still found it difficult to manage a sari, but her mother had insisted that she wear one to the temple.

'You're old enough now,' Sarada had said sternly. 'It isn't proper that you should go to do a puja with your bare legs showing.' She was often stern nowadays and rarely smiled or praised Neela, even when she did extra chores around the house. Neela tried to tell herself that it was because her mother was worried about Baba, but it still hurt.

Even though it wasn't a special festival day, the temple was surprisingly crowded. Sarada asked someone what was going on.

'The Chatterjees are having a puja done because they have a new grandson,' the woman replied. 'They've invited friends and relatives from many villages!'

Neela and her mother made their way through the throng to the priest and handed him their offerings, along with some money, so that he would chant the appropriate prayers for them. Sarada wanted to talk to the priest, so Neela found an empty spot near a pillar and sat down. She gazed at the statue of the goddess, half-obscured by garlands of marigolds and red hibiscus and shrouded in smoke from incense sticks. Kali, the dark goddess, was known as the protectress of the good and the destroyer of evil. Neela bent her head and prayed to Kali to bless her family and keep them all safe, especially her father. 'And Samar, also,' she whispered very softly. When she looked up, it seemed to her that the eyes of the deity were full of kindness, and a ray of hope brightened her heart.

'Isn't your name Neela?'

Neela turned, startled. A woman was smiling down at her. It took her a moment to recognize the woman for whom she had poured water on Usha's wedding day. As before, the woman was dressed in a fine handloom sari, and she wore a lot of beautiful jewellery, but what Neela liked more was the sweetness of her smile. She hadn't seen too many smiles recently.

'Yes, I'm Neela,' she said, smiling back, wondering exactly who the woman was. She didn't live in their village—Neela knew that much. Maybe she was a relative of the Chatterjees.

'May I sit here and talk with you for a bit?' the woman asked.

'Yes, of course,' Neela said, pleasantly surprised. Grown women rarely took the time to talk to young girls—except to tell them what to do. Or more often, what they'd done wrong! But this woman seemed really interested in *her*! She wanted to know all about how Neela spent her day, and she didn't seem shocked to hear that Neela liked to go fishing and to climb trees. She said she was impressed by how far Neela had progressed with her studies. She commended her on taking such good care of the cattle, and added that Budhi sounded like a very intelligent animal.

'I'm fond of cows, too,' the woman said. 'In our home— I live in Jal Gram, just a couple of hours from here—we have quite a few cows, and each day, I mix their feed myself. I have a favourite calf, a milk-white six-month-old that I've named Moti. She follows me everywhere. The other day, she even tried to come into the house!'

They laughed together. Then the woman said, 'Would you like to come and visit me sometime?'

Neela nodded, excited at the thought of a journey, even a short one. 'I've always wanted to see new places,' she confessed to the woman. 'But I've never been anywhere outside this village. I'd have to ask my mother's permission, though.'

'Of course! Maybe I can talk to her myself. Let me see if she's finished with the priest.' The woman—Neela realized that she didn't know her name yet—pushed through the crowd to where her mother was sitting. They spoke together for a few minutes, and then Sarada beckoned to Neela.

'You go home,' she said, surprising Neela. 'I'll come in a little while. There's rice and lentils, and a cauliflower curry. Go ahead and eat if I'm late.'

❖

An hour had passed, and her mother still wasn't back. Neela was hungry, but she sat on the porch, waiting, reluctant to eat by herself. Eating was a family activity. It didn't seem right to do it alone. She thought of the time when all of them—her father, her mother, Usha, and herself, used to sit right here on the porch at the end of the day to have a snack, enjoying the cool evening breeze. Neela sighed. Now half of her little family was gone.

Just then, she heard the twang of an ektara. It was the baoul, carrying the small bundle that contained his few possessions, standing outside their wicker gate with a smile.

Neela jumped up and ran to him. Maybe he would have news of her father! 'I'm so glad to see you, Baoul dadu! I was feeling really lonely.'

'Why, child? Where are your parents?'

Neela's heart fell. The baoul didn't know about Hari Charan being away. 'Baba's been gone since the day after the wedding. And Ma's at the temple,' she said dejectedly. Then a happy thought came to her. 'Would you like to join me for lunch?'

'I'd love to, Granddaughter!' the minstrel smiled. 'I've a mighty hunger inside my belly, like a whole army of gnawing mice!'

Quickly, Neela wiped the porch with a damp rag, unrolled two mats, and poured water for the baoul to wash his hands. She arranged rice and curry on two brass plates, making sure there was enough left for Sarada. Luckily, her mother, who still wasn't used to cooking for just two people, always made too much.

Neela waited impatiently for the old man to take a few hungry mouthfuls. Then she said, 'Did you come from Calcutta? Do you know what's happening there?'

The baoul shook his head. 'I've come from Dhaka, across the river. I went there to see what the freedom fighters on the other side of Bengal were doing—and to fan the flames of their enthusiasm a little. I did hear some news of Calcutta while I was there. But nothing good, I'm afraid. There was a big march in Calcutta, with black flags, some weeks back, demanding that the British quit India. On the day of the march, the British authorities ordered their Gurkha soldiers to charge the demonstrators—peaceful though they were—with lathis, nightsticks. It was a terrible sight, I'm told. Many heads were cracked open—even those of old men! There was blood everywhere.' His eyes flashed with anger. 'The leaders protested, but the authorities ignored them. When some of the marchers started fighting back, they were arrested and thrown in jail, and—'

'Baba went to Calcutta to join that march!' Neela blurted out, her eyes filling with tears. 'We haven't heard from him since. What if he's injured, or—or—?' She couldn't bring herself to say the terrible word.

The baoul patted her hand. 'I don't think he's dead. You have to trust me about this—I have a sixth sense for such things.'

Neela looked at him doubtfully.

'But he may well be imprisoned,' the baoul said.

'We have to find him—and get him out!'

'It won't be easy. I hear the government isn't even allowing a trial for political prisoners, to judge if they're guilty or innocent. They're just deporting them in droves to the Andaman prison colony, out in the middle of the ocean, so that they'll be out of the way—'

Just then, the gate creaked. It was Sarada.

'Neela!' she called out, smiling. 'I have some wonderful news for you! You'll never guess—'

Then her eyes fell on the baoul. 'What are you doing here?' she said with a frown. 'You're not supposed to come to this village anymore. Didn't Ram Prasad Chowdhury warn you? We'll get in trouble if his men see you at our house.'

'But, Ma—' Neela started.

'Don't interrupt me!' her mother snapped. To the baoul she said, 'Ram Prasad Chowdhury was right. You bring nothing but mischief! I know you're the reason my husband went off to Calcutta. Even though he pretended he was going on business, he couldn't fool me!'

Neela stared at her mother. All this time, she'd known!

'You made him feel guilty with your talk of freedom fighters,' Sarada was saying bitterly. 'And now—God alone knows what kind of difficulty he's in!'

The baoul looked at her with his kind, sad eyes. 'I know you're worried about your husband,' he said. 'I am, too. But great things are going on right now. The old empire is crumbling, and a new order will take its place, bringing us freedom. Brave, caring men like your husband want to be a part of this important moment—even though they know that when a huge structure falls, it crushes beneath it some of the people who helped to bring it down.'

'I don't understand all those poetic metaphors,' Sarada said in an angry voice. 'All I know is that my husband's missing—because he listened to talk like this! Can you bring him back? Can you? If not, I want you to be gone from my home!'

Neela gasped. This, from her mother, who was always telling her to be polite to her elders! But the minstrel stood up calmly. 'I will do as you wish. And I pray for your husband's safe return,' he said. He washed his hands and set off down the road, carrying his ektara and bundle.

'Ma!' Neela burst out accusingly. 'He didn't even finish eating!'

Her mother felt bad. Neela could tell that by looking at her face. She'd often told Neela that a guest was sacred and that it was bad luck if a guest went away hungry from your home. But all she said today was, 'I have a terrible headache. I'm going to lie down.'

'What was the news you had for me?' Neela asked as she started putting the food away. She didn't know what else to do.

'I'll tell you later. I'm too upset right now,' her mother said as she closed the bedroom door.

Neela put down the bundle on the steps of the ruined Krishna temple and wiped the sweat from her face. The afternoon sun was still very hot, but she hadn't wanted to wait until her mother woke up. She looked into the shadows of the ruin worriedly. Had she run all this way for nothing?

No, there he was, the baoul, lying down in the peaceful shade of a pillar.

'Baoul dadu,' Neela called, 'I saved your lunch and brought it for you.'

The baoul sat up. 'You shouldn't have done that, Granddaughter. Your mother will be angry with you.'

'But you didn't get to finish eating, mostly because I kept asking you questions. I felt so bad—I knew how hungry you were! And Ma—I'm sorry for what she said. I think she felt bad, too, afterward.'

'I don't blame your mother—and you must not, either,' the baoul said. 'This is a hard time for her.' He opened the bundle and took out the food Neela had wrapped for him in banana leaves. For a few minutes there was silence as he ate with relish.

'I've brought you some milk from Budhi,' Neela said, handing him a small pitcher. He drank it down to the last drop and gave a satisfied sigh.

'Thank you! That is the sweetest milk I've had in a long while.'

Now Neela voiced the question she had been waiting to ask all this time. 'Baoul dadu, how can we help my father?'

The baoul thought for a few minutes. Then he said, 'It's time I went back to Calcutta. I'll go and make some discreet inquiries.'

'Maybe the freedom fighters can help you—you know,

the group that came here?' Quickly, Neela told him about Samar and the note he had left.

The baoul nodded. 'That is an excellent idea! Biren is a good man, and brave, too! I'll contact Samar's cousin Bimala once I get to Calcutta, so she can put me in touch with them. But before I go, let me teach you the song you wanted to learn—*Vande Mataram!* I promised you I'd do that.'

The minstrel sang the words, and Neela sang them after him, picking up the tune effortlessly. Her voice was pure and sweet, and he nodded in approval.

'You have a real gift, child! I hope that we will gain our freedom soon, so I can come back and teach you more songs. In the meantime, I'll look for your father.'

Before she left, Neela sang the song once more, alone this time.

> *You are the strength in our arms, Mother.*
> *You are the devotion in our heart.*
> *We worship you! We worship you!*
> *We worship you throughout the land!*

The words resonated inside her all the way home.

Neela hurried into her room, on tiptoe. She would have liked to go wash up, but she was afraid the sound of the pump would wake her mother. So she lay on her bed, sweaty but pleased with the afternoon's work. The baoul had said that there was a train that stopped at Shona Gram at six in the morning. He would get on it and go to Calcutta—and find out where her father was.

'And if he *is* imprisoned—well, I'll do my best to get him out,' the baoul had assured her.

Neela felt good about that promise. Deep in her heart, she felt that there was more to the baoul than most people suspected. She wouldn't be surprised if he *did* bring her father back. She wouldn't be surprised at all! With a smile on her face, she dozed off.

She must have slept for quite a while, for the shadows outside her bedroom window had grown long when she awoke to the sound of knocks on the door. For a moment, terrified, she thought the constables had returned. Then she heard the voice of Ramu, the half-witted son of the village goatherd, calling her.

She ran to the door. 'Hush, Ramu! You know Ma doesn't like all this shouting. What is it?'

'I have something for you,' the boy said. He handed her a note and a bundle. She recognized the bundle right away—it was the baoul's. Why did Ramu have it? With a rapidly beating heart, she read the note:

My child, soon after you left, I learned from trusted sources that the police are looking for me. But my country needs me too much for me to rot in a British jail—perhaps for years! So for now, I must go into hiding. This means I cannot go to Calcutta, as we had planned, to find your father. You must do it yourself! Don't be afraid—you are stronger than you think. And there will be people to help you. *Vande Mataram*!

Neela's heart sank as she read the note.

'Neela, who's that at the door?' her mother called from the kitchen.

'Go, Ramu!' Neela whispered. She pushed him away gently and shut the door. Then she shouted, 'It was Ramu—he stopped by to see if we wanted to buy one of his father's goats.'

'What a silly boy!' Sarada said. 'It's almost night—is this the time to be bringing around goats for sale?' She seemed to have recovered some of her good humour.

Neela felt guilty about deceiving her mother, but she didn't know what else she could do. So much had happened so quickly. Her head was whirling. She needed to be alone to think about the baoul's note. But her mother was calling her.

'Come, Neela, let me comb your hair for you. It's time I told you the wonderful news.'

As she ran the comb through Neela's hair, Sarada told her about the woman at the temple, who was, indeed, a friend of the Chatterjees. Her name was Sarojini Misra, and she was the wife of a rich businessman in Jal Gram. And she wanted Neela to be her daughter-in-law!

Neela was too stunned to say anything, but Sarada didn't seem to notice. 'She really liked you,' she went on excitedly, 'from seeing you at Usha's wedding and from talking to you today. I asked the Chatterjees' daughter about her, and she said she's a really kind person, very well respected in Jal Gram. And so well off! Why, Neela, you'll be able to have everything you want! Her son is an educated young man—he studied for a year in college, even. He helps his father run the family business. He sounds very pleasant—'

'But, Ma,' Neela managed to whisper, 'I'm much too young! I don't want to get married at all.'

'Don't worry,' her mother said. 'The Misras are not in a rush. The wedding can take place in a couple of years. But there's a really lucky day coming up in a couple of weeks, and they want to go ahead with a small engagement ceremony.'

'But, Ma, I haven't even seen her son—'

'Ah yes! I've invited their whole family over the day after tomorrow for lunch. That way everyone can get to see everyone—'

'But what about Baba?' Neela cried. Surely if her father were here, he wouldn't be rushing her into an engagement! Though she had liked the woman, Neela was just not ready for such a big step.

'It's most unfortunate that your father isn't here,' Sarada said sadly. 'But I know he wouldn't want us to let such a good match slip through our fingers. Why, it's not every day a rich and cultured family wants to form a marriage alliance with your daughter!' Her voice was firm, and Neela knew her mother wouldn't change her mind.

Alone in her room, Neela gave in to tears. What was she going to do? An engagement ceremony was a serious thing. Once it was completed, she couldn't back out of it. *Engaged girls are kept under strict supervision and expected to behave properly at all times. It would be the end of whatever little freedom I have!* She wished she had someone to discuss her problems with—someone like Samar. *But now I'll never see Samar again. And what about Baba, spending his days in misery in some hateful British jail? Who will rescue him?* These thoughts made her weep even more.

After some time, though, Neela grew tired of crying. She opened the bundle Ramu had brought, to see what the baoul had left for her. Inside was a minstrel's outfit—a longish saffron robe and a turban cloth. But why would he give these to her?

Without thinking, Neela slipped on the robe. On the baoul, it had been calf-length. On her, it reached to her ankles. But—here she was glad that she'd been practicing wearing a sari—she could walk in it without tripping. She bundled up her long hair and tied the turban tightly over it. Slowly, an idea began to form in her mind.

Alone in a City of Strangers

Neela woke before dawn and put on the clothes the baoul had left for her. She tiptoed to the kitchen where her mother kept the housekeeping money in an old earthenware jar, and took from it a handful of rupee notes. *I'm sorry, Ma,* she said to her mother silently. *But I'm sure if you knew why I was taking it, you wouldn't mind.*

The hardest part was writing the letter. She had to choose simple words, because her mother couldn't read very well. After several tries, she finally wrote:

> *Dear Ma,*
> *I'm going to Calcutta to look for Baba and bring him back. Please don't worry. I will be very, very careful.*
> *Your loving daughter*

She slipped out of the house while it was still dark and ran all the way to the station. She had no clock, and she was afraid she would miss the train. But she was one of the first to arrive at the platform. She stood to one side, her face turned away from the few fellow passengers travelling this early. When it was time to get her ticket, she was scared that the clerk at the counter would recognize her. *Will my voice give me away as a girl?* she wondered. But when she asked for a one-way ticket to Calcutta, he merely yawned and pushed the small cardboard rectangle across the counter without even glancing at her face.

Neela stared out the window as the train picked up speed, shading her eyes carefully so the coal dust from the steam engine would not get into them. It seemed to her that she had been on the train for a very long time.

'How much further is it to Calcutta?' she asked the man sitting next to her.

'Just a few more minutes,' he said, twirling his moustache, 'and we'll reach Howrah Station. Boy, is this your first trip to the city?'

'Oh, no!' Neela said, resisting an impulse to fiddle with her robe and turban. She repeated the words she had practised to herself earlier. 'I've been here before. I have relatives in Calcutta.'

She hoped the man would leave her alone, but he asked, with friendly curiosity, 'Where do they live?'

'Near Park Street,' Neela said reluctantly. It was one of the only two street names she knew, or else she would have given a different one.

'Really?' the man raised his eyebrows. 'That's a very

fancy part of town. A lot of the British sahibs live there, and some very rich Indians.' His expression indicated that he didn't see how the relatives of a baoul—who, though holy, was after all little more than a beggar—could live in such an expensive neighbourhood.

'My aunt,' Neela said, thinking quickly, 'she's—uh—a maid in a rich man's house.'

'I see!' The man, satisfied, went back to reading his paper, the *Amrita Bazaar Patrika*.

The train came to a halt with a screech of brakes, and Neela followed the other passengers out of the compartment. She looked around at the huge station in stupefaction. Unlike the station at Shona Gram, which was nothing more than a raised gravel platform and a small ticket booth, this was an enclosed area, its vaulted ceilings reaching almost to the sky. *I didn't expect it to be this big—or this crowded!* she thought. People milled around, pushing past each other to get to the exit. Everyone seemed to be in such a hurry. And the noise! Vendors shouted their wares, announcements were made on a booming megaphone, the huge station clock chimed the hour, and steam engines blew their whistles.

A coolie in a red uniform yelled, 'Out of the way, you country bumpkin!' as he ran by with a trunk on his head, shoving Neela so hard that she almost fell.

How will I ever find my way out of all of this to get to Milford Lane? she wondered.

The crush of people carried Neela toward the big exit doors. But outside it was just as confusing. There were more vendors—so many that it seemed like a pavement market—selling everything from food to clothing to pots and pans to miracle cures for all kinds of diseases. Families of beggars, several of them missing limbs, huddled on mats. There were all kinds of transportation—big red buses, and vehicles that looked like two train cars joined together and connected to wires that crackled overhead. *Those must be the trams Baba told me about,* thought Neela. There were carriages of various kinds—shiny black ones pulled by four horses; dowdy, covered ones pulled by mules; and even rickshaws pulled by men. Neela looked around, confused. *Which one should I take?*

'What's the matter, boy? Lost?' a voice spoke next to her ear. It was the man from the train, grinning at her confusion.

'It's been a while since I was here last,' Neela said defensively. 'Everything looks so different.'

'Ah, yes, that's Calcutta for you! Blink, and there'll be something new,' the man said proudly, as though he was personally responsible for every change. He pointed her toward a tram marked 'Alipore', which stood behind a long line of other trams. 'Tell the conductor to let you off at the corner of Park Street,' he told her. 'You can walk from there.'

'Oh yes, that's the one,' said Neela, pretending to recognize the tram. 'Thank you!'

Neela climbed onto the tram and bought a ticket from the uniformed conductor for a few coins. She moved automatically toward a seat marked 'Ladies' but stopped herself just in time, and then took a seat by a window. The tram filled up fast, and with a clanging of bells, they were on their way.

As the tram crossed a bridge to enter the actual city of Calcutta, Neela stared up at the shining metal girders. It was the largest structure she had ever seen. It looked so solid, she couldn't believe that it was raised each day to let ships from the Khidderpore Docks pass through to the ocean, as her father had told her. The streets of Calcutta, broad and crowded with vehicles, people, and even animals, were paved with black pitch. She remembered Samar mentioning how the pitch would melt on a very hot day and stick to his feet. The buildings lining the streets were huge and stately, with massive pillars and large green-shuttered windows. Many had balconies with wrought-iron railings shaped into intricate designs. Some, set back farther from the road and surrounded by trees, looked like fancy homes. Elsewhere, there were factories spewing black smoke, and dark, narrow alleys leading away from the tramlines, where garbage was piled up. They passed churches, and a tall monument in the centre of a huge field, and something that looked like a palace.

How many people, rich and poor, must live in such a huge city, the capital of British India! Neela thought, her heart sinking. *How will I ever find Samar here?* For a moment she wished she were back in the familiar safety of her village.

'Pull yourself together!' she said to herself sternly. 'You can't give up even before you've started.'

She got off the tram at the corner of Park Street, which did, indeed, look like a very fancy area of town. Shiny motor cars driven by men in uniforms sped noisily down the broad street, which was lined with large, cream-coloured mansions. Many of the cars carried white passengers. *Those must be the British,* thought Neela, trying to peer into a car that had stopped at a crossing. But except for their pink skin and unusual clothes—the men in trousers and coats, the women in long, belted dresses and hats—they looked just like anyone else. Why did the freedom fighters hate them so much?

'Hey, you!' shouted the chauffeur of the car. 'What are you staring at? *Hatho! Hatho!* Move!'

'Damn beggars!' exclaimed the white man in the back seat to his companion, his lips twisted in a sneer. 'Can't get away from them anywhere in this city. They should all be whipped.'

Neela flinched back, her face burning. The man had spoken with such disgust—as though he didn't consider people like her to be human beings. She became very aware of her old clothes and bare feet, here on a street where everyone was so well dressed.

At the same time she was furious. *How dare he speak to me like that! This isn't even his country!* She remembered Samar saying that the British had come here merely as traders with the East India Company and had taken control of India through trickery. *And now they think they are better than the Indians!* For the first time,

Neela began to really understand why the freedom fighters were willing to risk their lives for independence.

Neela wandered for a while, aware of the suspicious looks passersby were giving her. She saw many streets leading off from Park Street, but none of them was the one she was looking for. She was beginning to get hungry and tired. Her feet were sore from walking on the stone pavement, so much rougher and harder than the dirt roads of home. It was late afternoon already, and she hadn't eaten all day. She wished she had picked up some roasted peanuts and puffed rice from the vendors at Howrah Station. There were restaurants and cakeshops on Park Street, but Neela knew, instinctively, that she couldn't go into them even though she had the money.

Finally, in an alleyway, Neela saw a man unloading a wheelbarrow. He must have been bringing supplies to one of the stores. He was the first person she had seen on this street dressed in Indian clothes and with a turban around his head that didn't look so different from hers.

'Do you know where Milford Lane is?' she asked him hesitantly. She was lucky. He pointed it out to her.

'You'd better go around to the back of the house,' he advised after she mentioned that her aunt worked there. 'These rich people—they don't like servants coming to their front gate.'

The house at 99 Milford Lane was an imposing mansion, and Neela stared at it from across the road, feeling intimidated. There were tall pillars all the way across the front of the three-storey house, and a big marble entrance. Beyond the tall wrought-iron gates, where a gatekeeper sat on a stool, colourful beds of flowers filled the extensive gardens. Water from a white fountain shaped like a giant fish sparkled merrily in the sun.

Finally she gathered up enough courage to cross the street and talk to the gatekeeper.

'I'm a—friend of Bimala's,' she said hesitantly. 'Can you please tell her that I would like to see her?'

The gatekeeper looked her up and down with disbelief.

'A friend indeed!' he scoffed. 'And what would Bimala memsahib be wanting with a friend like you?'

'She—I—'

'Make yourself scarce!' the man said, gesturing with his stick. 'I don't know how you found out her name! Maybe from hanging around the back entrance and listening to the servants gossiping. You'd better get away before the master, her father, sees you, or you'll be in real trouble—and so will I!'

'Please—I have to see her!' Neela pleaded, on the point of tears.

The gatekeeper was adamant. 'Get away! Didn't you hear me? Or you'll be getting a box on the ears!' He shoved her, and she fell against the compound wall and scraped her arm.

Neela moved away and sat down on the hard concrete pavement, at her wit's end. The gatekeeper was shaking his fist, telling her to be gone if she knew what was good for her. *But where can I go?* she thought.

Just then a shiny black car pulled up near her. Neela scrambled up to see who was in there, but from where she stood, she couldn't see much. It must have been someone important, though, because the gatekeeper stood tall, with a smart salute, and opened the gates. The car was almost inside when Neela heard a voice call, 'Wait! Who's that?'

A young woman of about eighteen years had lowered the car window and was looking at Neela with a frown. She was very pretty and was fashionably dressed in a sari made of a thin, gauzy material that looked like dragonfly wings, with a matching blouse with very short sleeves. Diamonds sparkled in her ears.

'Nothing, nothing, Bimala memsahib!' the gatekeeper said hurriedly. 'Just a street urchin, begging for food. I'll make sure he leaves right away.'

Bimala nodded and began to put up her window. The car started moving again.

Neela ran up to the car, dodging the yelling gatekeeper. She was terrified, but this was her only chance. 'I'm not a street urchin,' she shouted. 'I'm Samar's friend. He told me to come to you.'

The car came to a halt. The window was lowered again.

'Samar's friend?' Bimala said, staring at Neela. When Neela nodded, Bimala opened the door and motioned to her to get in. The seat was covered with a maroon, velvety material, and there was a maroon carpet on the floor of the car. Neela looked down at her dirty feet and hesitated.

'It doesn't matter,' Bimala said impatiently. 'Come on, get in!'

The chauffeur and the gatekeeper were both protesting loudly. 'You mustn't let a stranger into the house, memsahib!' the gatekeeper cried, wringing his hands. 'Who knows what harm he intends? Master will be furious if he hears of it.'

'Then we must make sure Master doesn't hear of it, mustn't we?' said Bimala with a cool smile as she put the window up again.

Neela followed Bimala inside. They entered a room that was richly furnished with dark mahogany settees and an easy chair with a cushioned footstool. There were huge paintings on the walls. One of them was of a wrinkled old white woman in a crown and a long puffy dress. Neela stared at it.

'Queen Victoria,' Bimala said with a smile that Neela couldn't quite figure out. Bimala shut the door behind her. 'She used to be in the big drawing room, until she died. Now that room has a picture of George VI, our current monarch. We're very careful to keep up with the times, you see!'

Neela couldn't help staring at Bimala, too. She was so elegant with her stylish clothes and jewellery. She wore a tiny wristwatch, carried a purse, and wore shoes with little heels. She was the first woman Neela had seen who wore shoes! *Could this fashionable young woman really be the caring cousin Samar had described?* Neela asked herself.

Bimala had dropped into the easy chair and kicked off her shoes. As Neela watched, she removed her silk ankle socks and threw them on the floor with a grimace. 'Ah! That's better!' she said, wiggling her toes. 'I wish Papa wouldn't insist on me wearing those outlandish things. They're so hot and uncomfortable. But he wants us to be "cultured", like his British friends. Tell me now, what news do you have of Samar? Is he all right? I worry about that hotheaded cousin of mine!' An affectionate look had replaced the haughty expression on her face.

Quickly, Neela explained that she had come to Calcutta to search for her father and that Samar had given her Bimala's address. 'I was hoping you could help me get in touch with him,' she ended.

Bimala looked both disappointed and doubtful. 'He did give me the address of a small grocery, a place where I could leave word for him, but the last couple of times I did that, he never got back to me. I have a feeling that he might be away from Calcutta on an assignment.'

'But Samar was injured, and I—we—helped him, at least until the authorities came. He got away, but what if he couldn't get back here? What'll I do about my father?' Neela was distraught.

'Don't lose heart,' Bimala said, her voice sympathetic. 'And thank you for helping Samar. For now, I'll send Bishu, my personal attendant, with a message. Maybe we'll get lucky this time—maybe Samar's back. Bishu can also ask around about your father. Don't look so worried! Bishu's been with our family from before I was born— he's more of a friend and adviser than an attendant to me. I'd trust him with my life. What's your name, by the way?'

Neela hesitated. Then she said, 'Uh—it's Neela.'

'What?' Bimala's voice was disbelieving.

In response, Neela took off her turban and shook out her long hair.

Bimala stared at her for what seemed like a very long time. *Was she angry at being tricked?* Neela worried. But then Bimala burst out laughing.

'Goodness! You certainly had me fooled!' she said. 'This is getting more and more interesting! You must tell me all about yourself—how you came to be dressed like this, how you met Samar. But first, let's get you some proper girls' clothes, and something to eat. You'd probably like a bath, too, wouldn't you? Oh yes, we'll also have to figure out a good story to tell Papa—so he doesn't throw you out of the house. We are going to have such fun! And don't worry, we'll find both Samar and your father in the bargain.'

Still laughing, she took Neela by the hand and led her upstairs.

A Desperate Search

Neela poured the last mugful of warm water over herself and sighed luxuriously. Then she wiped herself with a thick towel and looked around once more. If she hadn't seen it with her own eyes, she wouldn't have believed that a room like this could exist!

Bimala's bathroom had a white sink and shiny brass taps with running water. A huge bathtub with feet like a bird's claws sat in one corner of the room. A pretty soap dish, decorated with more pictures of white women in puffy dresses, held a big bar of scented soap.

Neela had sniffed the air appreciatively when she entered the bathroom. 'What's that smell? It's so lovely—and different.'

'Lavender,' Bimala had said. 'Papa buys it from a store in Hogg's Market that specializes in British goods.' Her eyes had clouded. 'Samar used to get really upset about that when he lived here. Personally, I'd rather not be using all this foreign stuff, especially when the freedom fighters have asked all Indians to boycott them, but Papa doesn't agree. And I can't fight with him all the time.'

Now that she was clean, Neela slipped on the dress that Bimala had loaned her. It was pale pink, with lace at the neck and cuffs and pearly buttons down the front. The waist was gathered and had a sash that tied into a bow in the back. The dress reached down to her calves and had a soft pink petticoat of the finest linen. To complete the outfit, Bimala had given her a pair of black leather shoes with shiny silver buckles.

Bimala was waiting for her eagerly, standing outside the bathroom door.

'You look great!' she exclaimed, clapping her hands as Neela came out.

'It's much too fine,' Neela protested guiltily. Part of her guilt was because the dress was obviously foreign-made.

'Oh, don't be silly!' Bimala said. 'It was just gathering dust in my cupboard since I outgrew it. And I'm sure Papa won't recognize it. Think of it as a disguise. You've got to fit the role we've thought up for you! Now—do you remember all the details?'

Neela nodded. 'I'm supposed to be a cousin of one of your classmates from Lady Brabourne College. I came from my home in the countryside to spend a week with my cousin in Calcutta, only to find that she and her family have come down with the chicken pox. Since it's so contagious, their doctor said that I should not stay with them. My cousin contacted you, and you kindly brought me home to stay with you for a few days—if your father allows it.'

'Excellent,' Bimala said. 'Now if only I can keep myself

from giggling as we tell all this to Papa!'

Limping a little because of her shoes, Neela felt her heart beat wildly as she walked behind Bimala to the dining room to meet her father. Surely the Honourable Lal Mohan Das, the eminent judge, would not be fooled by their story—especially when they started eating! Neela eyed the silverware set by her plates with dismay. At home she always ate with her hands, like most Indians. *How will I manage all these utensils, even if I watch Bimala carefully?* she wondered. *And what if the servants give me away?* Bimala had assured her that they were completely loyal to Bimala and would never do anything to get her into trouble with her father, as long as it didn't have anything directly to do with Samar, whom her father hated. Still, Neela was doubtful. *After all, didn't they hear me tell Bimala that I'm a friend of Samar's?*

But the servants didn't say a word, and Bimala's father must have been preoccupied, because he glanced only briefly at Neela, gave an absentminded nod, and patted Bimala's hand. 'I'm glad you have someone closer to your own age to spend time with,' he said. 'I know I haven't been very good company for you lately—I've had too much on my mind. It's especially at times like this that I wish your mother was still with us. I can never be as good a parent as she was to you.'

'Oh, Papa!' Bimala said, and from her face Neela could see that for all her criticism of her father's ways, she loved him dearly. 'Don't say that! You're a wonderful father. Is it a difficult case you're working on?'

'More terrorists to be deported,' her father said heavily, pushing away the mulligatawny soup the servant had set before him. 'There was another attempt on the governor general's life by a group of young men. Why, some of them must have been no more than sixteen years old! Has this country gone totally crazy? Gandhi's followers are bad enough, but these young people will stop at nothing!'

Neela tensed, and Bimala stared at her father, her face stricken, until he shook his head. 'No, Samar was not among them, that good-for-nothing! But if he were, you know I'd have to do my job, even if he is my own dead sister's son.'

Bimala nodded wordlessly, and they finished the rest of the four-course dinner in silence, though Neela hardly ate a thing.

The next morning Bimala's attendant, Bishu, went to leave a message for Samar at the grocery store. He was also going to stop at the Alipore Prison. An old friend of his worked in the kitchen there. 'I hear that a lot of the freedom fighters are being kept in that jail, Bimala memsahib,' he said. 'Let's see if I can find anything out. But don't hope for too much. Nowadays, most people are too scared to talk.'

Bimala had to go to her college classes soon after that, and Neela was left at home with no one to talk to. She paced the upstairs balcony restlessly. Bimala had told her to choose whichever books she wanted from the library and had shown her how to work the gramophone in the music room, but Neela was too worried to read or even to listen to the latest songs, which ordinarily she would have loved to do. *What if Bishu can't find out where Baba is?* she thought. *What if Baba isn't imprisoned but is lying wounded and ill somewhere else—too ill to send word to Shona Gram? What if he's dying? And even if he is in jail, how will we ever get him out? Samar might be somewhere far away—and even Samar is just a boy, really. What can he do against the entire British empire? And my poor mother back home—how frantic she must be with worry! And Budhi—who's taking care of her? She won't understand what has happened. She'll only moo sadly in distress, thinking that I've abandoned her.*

Neela wondered if everything she'd done so far was a mistake. Was it all going to be for nothing?

She laid her head on the edge of the balcony and wept.

Three days had passed, and they had heard nothing. Bishu's friend at the prison was willing to help, but he didn't know much. The prison cooks didn't have any contact with the prisoners. Also, almost no one working there knew the real identity of the prisoners, who were referred to only by the numbers stitched on their prison uniforms.

'Does your father have any distinguishing marks? A

mole on his face, maybe, or a birthmark?' Bimala asked Neela.

Neela shook her head. Then she remembered. 'He does have an old scar on the back of his left hand, shaped like a V.'

'I'll tell Bishu to let his friend know about it,' Bimala said.

But Bishu's friend wasn't able to get close enough to the prisoners to notice a scar.

Of Samar, there was no news at all.

'What shall we do now?' Neela asked Bimala.

Bimala shook her head dispiritedly. 'I can't think of anything else. We'll just have to wait.'

Waiting had always been hard for Neela, and this time it was even more so. She tossed and turned in bed all night. She dreamed of flames and floods, of her mother's face thin with worrying, of Budhi crying to be milked. In her dreams, her father called to her for help, and the beautiful, crowned woman—who was she?—beckoned sadly to her with silvery arms. There were dark circles under Neela's eyes when she awoke, and she could hardly eat any of the fancy dishes that Bimala's cook served them. She looked so dejected that even Bimala's father noticed and asked if she were feeling homesick.

'You mustn't sit in the house and mope, my dear,' he said to her kindly, 'even if your cousin is ill and you can't spend time with her. Calcutta is such a fine city. There's so much to see and learn. Make the most of your time here.' He turned to his daughter. 'Bimala, why don't you take your friend out and about tomorrow? Maybe she would like to go shopping. And she'd probably enjoy going with you to that Drama Club you like so much—don't you have a performance coming up soon?'

'Yes, Papa, the dress rehearsal's in just two days,' Bimala said.

'I'm sure that Neela would like to see that. What are you putting on this time?'

'A dance drama based on one of Tagore's poems.'

'Ah, yes, Tagore!' Bimala's father nodded approvingly. 'Very elegant. No wonder he received the Nobel prize! Now, let's see, tomorrow I can send the chauffeur back after he drops me at court, and you can have the car all day. Neela, my child, try a little of this egg custard—it really is very good.'

His words brought a lump to Neela's throat. She hadn't expected such kindness from the man who had been so harsh with Samar and who, she had learned, was known as such a ruthless judge. How many sides there were to people! Before he went to bed, he would give Bimala a kiss on her cheek and lay his hand on her head for a quiet moment—much like Neela's own father might have done. And the other day, she had seen him quietly passing a stack of rupee bills to the cook, whose sick son had to be taken to the hospital. *I'd been prepared to hate him,* she thought, *but I can't!*

The next day Bimala took Neela sightseeing. They drove by the racecourse, with its many-coloured flags, and walked along the cobbled footpath at Outram Ghat, shaded by pipal trees, where the Hooghly River curves in a wide arc on its way to the sea. They shopped for trinkets among the colourful, crowded storefronts of Bara Bazaar, where Neela bought a pair of white conch shell bangles for her mother, and they offered prayers at Kali Ghat, the famous temple of the Goddess Kali. But Neela was distracted and hardly even enjoyed the pistachio ice cream Bimala bought for her—even though it was the first time she had ever tasted ice cream.

'Cheer up!' Bimala said to her when they returned home. 'You've got to be patient! Complicated things take time to achieve.'

But Neela had a feeling that time was running out.

'How about a cup of hot tea? That always makes me feel better when I'm sad. I'll ask the servant to bring it to us on the front balcony above the entrance. Then we can watch the passersby as we drink.'

Hot ginger tea, fruitcake, and spicy potato-filled singaras were brought to them on the balcony. As they sipped and munched, they heard a commotion at the gate. A bearded man stood outside, arguing with the gatekeeper. Like most street vendors, he wore a loose kurta and dhoti, but he didn't carry any wares. Instead, he held a drum, and on his shoulder sat a tiny monkey dressed in a velvet cap and jacket.

Bimala clapped her hands. 'Oh, it's a monkey-dance man! Have you ever seen one? Their monkeys know the most amazing tricks!'

When Neela shook her head, Bimala called out to the

gatekeeper. 'Oh, Darwan, tell the man to come inside the gate. We want to see the monkey perform.'

Grumbling, the gatekeeper motioned to the man to enter. The man grinned, stroking his thick moustache. Bowing deeply to the girls, he began to play on his drum. He sang a funny song about a monkey's wedding, while his pet danced, somersaulted, and even juggled a couple of balls.

'He's very good,' Neela said. As the monkey—and the man—winked at them in unison, she laughed for the first time in days.

'Wait!' Bimala gripped Neela's hand. 'I think—'

'What?'

Bimala shook her head. 'I'm just not sure,' she muttered.

'Will the ladies give my poor monkey and me a few paise to buy some food?' the man called in broken street Hindi.

'Yes,' Bimala said. But instead of throwing the money down from the balcony, as Neela expected her to, she ran down the stairs. As she handed the man a rupee note, Bimala stared at him intently. Then, suddenly, she gave an excited cry and hugged him!

'Bimala didi,' the man said in a different, laughing voice—a voice that Neela recognized. 'Control yourself! You're going to give me away!'

❖

Samar—for it was he under the false beard and moustache that made him look so much older—could only stay a little while.

'It isn't safe,' he said, and Bimala agreed.

Bimala hurried him and Neela inside. 'Tell him everything while I go talk to the gatekeeper,' she said. 'I'll have to make up a good story—the servants all have express orders to inform my father immediately if Samar dares to return here. That's why I haven't seen him in ages. I'd better get some food, too. Poor Samar looks as if he hasn't eaten in days.'

'Not days, Bimala didi, weeks!' Samar said with a mock sigh. 'Do you think you could cajole the cook into frying up some of those wonderful, crisp luchis he used to make for us? Or does he only fix Yorkshire pudding nowadays?'

Neela laughed as Bimala gave him a playful cuff on the ear before leaving.

Samar looked at Neela, serious again. 'Tell me, what has brought you to Calcutta? And why are you here, at my cousin's?'

'It's my father—he never returned to Shona Gram.' Neela couldn't keep back the tears as she confided her fears about her father to him. She also found herself telling him how much she missed her home and her mother. Samar patted her arm awkwardly.

'Don't worry! We'll think of something, Bimala and you and I—and Biren. I must tell him. He's good at coming up with plans.'

Bimala had returned with a plateful of the puffy fried

bread, along with a potato-and-cauliflower curry, a big glass of milk, and a couple of bananas for Samar's monkey. She nodded reassuringly at Neela.

Neela felt the tears rising to her eyes once more. 'I'm so thankful to have generous friends like you,' she said.

'Please! Don't say anything!' Samar said. 'You did much more than this for me.' He turned to Bimala. 'I'll have to tell you *that* story another day. Now listen carefully. I won't be able to come here again. It's too risky. You must send Bishu to the grocery the day after tomorrow. I'll have a message waiting there for him.'

Carefully, after checking to make sure none of the servants were around, Bimala let Samar out through a side door that faced an alleyway.

'Be careful!' she entreated, biting her lip.

He gave her a hug. 'You know I will. I've no intention of dying and missing out on your wedding feast! The only question is, who's going to marry someone as ugly as you?'

The girls couldn't help smiling. Samar gave Neela's hand a quick squeeze. '*Vande Mataram*!' he whispered. How handsome and brave his face looked in the flickering light from the gas streetlamp!

'*Vande Mataram*!' she whispered back, feeling more hopeful than she had in weeks.

A Daring Plan

'Wake up, sleepyhead!'

Neela sat up in confusion, rubbing her tired eyes. She had lain awake much of the night, wondering what kind of plan Biren and Samar could possibly come up with. She had fallen into a restless sleep only after the night watchman, who patrolled the streets banging rhythmically with his lathi on the cobblestones, had called out that it was three o'clock.

For a moment, Neela thought she was back home in the village, and in her own cot. Had she merely dreamed, then, of her visit to Calcutta and of her father's disappearance? Her heart soared. Any moment now, Ma would call her to milk Budhi! But then she realized that the bed was too soft and luxurious, with its muslin sheets and its carved footboard. And that wasn't her mother's voice waking her up.

'I never knew a girl who could sleep so much!' Bimala's voice teased her. 'I need to talk to you before I go to my classes—I have some news! No, not from Biren—it's too early for that. This is from Bishu's friend, the one who works at the prison.'

Neela held her breath.

Bimala dropped her voice to a whisper. 'Yesterday, some of the guards who serve lunch to the prisoners were sick with influenza, so Bishu's friend was ordered to serve. He watched the prisoners carefully as he filled their bowls—and he saw that one of them had a scar, like a V, on his hand. When Bishu's friend was about to serve the prisoner, he dropped his ladle on purpose. As he bent to pick it up, he asked, very softly, if he was Hari Charan from Shona Gram—and the man nodded!'

'Baba!' Neela cried, almost too happy to believe it. 'But are you sure?'

'Shhh! I think so! I've already sent Bishu to the grocery, so the go-between can let Biren and Samar know this.'

'Oh, thank you, Bimala!' Neela whispered, gripping Bimala's hands in hers. 'At least I know he's alive. Did he say if Baba looked all right?'

'Bishu's friend said that your father was very thin, had a dirty bandage around his head, and walked with a limp. But he didn't seem ill, not like some of the others, who have fevers and cough up blood—'

Neela blinked back tears at the thought of her strong, confident father walking with a limp. *But it could be a lot worse,* she told herself resolutely. *At least now I know he's alive.*

'There's something else,' Bimala added. 'Bishu's friend went into the guards' quarters to bring gruel to the men who were sick, and he overheard the guards saying that a large group of prisoners was going to be deported tonight.'

'Tonight!' Neela cried in dismay.

'Keep your voice down!' Bimala hissed. 'We don't want any of the servants to overhear us and tell Papa—which they surely would, if they thought I was getting involved in something dangerous. Anyway, Biren knows this, too. We'll just have to trust him and see what he decides to do.'

She looked at the impatience on Neela's face and smiled. 'I know it's hard for you to wait, so I've brought you something to read. It's the poem by Tagore that our Drama Club is performing. Tonight is our dress rehearsal, remember? When I get back from college, you can help me practise my part.'

Neela had lunch by herself, barely picking at the fish fries with tomato sauce that the cook brought her, so that he clicked his tongue in disapproval. After lunch she went to the music room with the poem Bimala had given her.

The poem was titled *Bashab Datta*, and it was about a beautiful dancing girl from ancient times, Bashab Datta, who falls in love with a young monk. She invites him to her home, but the monk refuses, saying that the time is not right, but that he will certainly come to her one day. Years pass, the dancer falls ill with smallpox, and the townspeople, afraid of catching the disease, put her outside the walls of the city. She lies there, delirious and alone, preparing to die—when a stranger comes and nurses her with great love and compassion. It is the monk!

Neela liked the way the poem gave her a sense of a different place and time. Tagore's words were powerful and evocative, painting pictures inside her closed eyelids. *I can almost see the beautiful dancer walking home at night after a performance,* she thought, *her anklets chiming, the lantern in her hand throwing a brief glow around her. And the noble monk, who came back to take care of the dancer after she was ill and disfigured—I can see him, too!* She imagined that he looked a little bit like Samar.

But her mind was too restless for her to focus on the poem for long, and she started flipping through some of the records that filled the shelves of the music room. There were so many songs here that she hadn't even heard of— religious songs about the Goddess Kali by a singer named Ram Prasad, songs by Tagore, and more by a singer called Rajani Kanta. There was a record of folk songs by baouls of Bengal. With a pang, Neela thought of her own baoul. *Wherever he is, I hope he's safe!*

Maybe it was because she was thinking of him that she started humming, almost without realizing what she was doing.

'Vande Mataram!' she sang softly to herself, closing her eyes to remember the words better.

> *Beautiful Mother, bathed in silver moonlight,*
> *lovely as a lake filled with lotuses,*
> *I owe you my very life!*

When she finished, there was a moment of total silence,

and then the sound of clapping came from the door. Startled, Neela whirled around, her heart pounding. *What trouble am I getting myself into now?* she thought. *This is a banned song, and here I am singing it in the home of a staunch supporter of the British empire!* But luckily, it was Bimala.

'Thank God it's only you!' Neela said, relieved.

'You sing so beautifully,' Bimala said. 'And the song, too, is so powerful. I've never heard it before—though, of course, I'd heard about it. It makes me understand a bit of how Samar must feel. Sometimes I wish I could—' She stopped and shook her head as though to clear it of thoughts she shouldn't be thinking. 'Enough! We need to focus on what needs to be done. Bishu just brought back a message from the grocery. Here, let's read it together.'

The note was brief and unsigned. It read:

N—
Be at the intersection of Rajmohan and Belgachi roads tonight at eleven. Come alone. B must not get involved in this any further.

'I never get to do anything exciting!' Bimala said, stamping her foot in annoyance. But after a moment she sighed. 'Samar's right. It would cause a great scandal for my father if I got caught trying to free prisoners that he had sentenced! But let me think now, where are these streets? I don't recognize the names. Let's ask Bishu.'

Bishu informed them that the two roads were small side streets near the docks. Neela clasped her hands. 'That must be the route the army lorry is supposed to use to get the prisoners to the docks tonight!' she said.

Together they decided that Neela would accompany Bimala that evening to the dress rehearsal at the Drama Club. On the way back, Bimala would tell the driver to drop Neela at the intersection mentioned in the note. Bishu would be waiting for her there. He would stay with her until Samar came.

'Don't worry,' Bimala said as she tore the note into tiny pieces and gave them to Bishu to burn. 'I'm sure Biren has planned the next stage very carefully.' But her face was uncertain, and Neela could tell that she wasn't sure of it at all.

The members of the Drama Club were, like Bimala, the daughters of rich, old Calcutta families who did not want their children getting involved in anything as messy as politics. For the most part, the children didn't want it either, as Neela could clearly see by all the imported clothing, shoes, and make-up they wore. Their manners were affected and Western—and, Neela thought, quite comical, as they shook hands and said 'How do you do?' to each other. Their talk—peppered with fancy English phrases— was mostly about new fashions, upcoming parties, who was getting engaged to whom, and, of course, the latest high-society scandals.

Bimala took Neela around the room and introduced her to all her friends. But the young women didn't pay much attention to Neela, once they figured out that she didn't belong to an important Calcutta family. Neela didn't mind. It amused her to listen and watch as they gossiped and flitted around busily, or changed into their stage costumes.

Most of them were enrolled in women's colleges, but Neela thought they seemed less interested in books than in landing rich husbands. *Why,* she thought in surprise as she listened to them heatedly discussing a new hairstyle they'd seen in a British magazine, *even I know more about the world than they do! I wonder if Bimala would have been like that, too, if Samar hadn't made her realize that there was more to life than fancy jewellery and French perfume.*

Bimala, in addition to playing the dancer's role, was in charge of doing the make-up. Neela watched with fascination as Bimala transformed the Drama Club members into wrinkled old men and women, a jewelled, haughty queen, a palace guard with a thick moustache, and a monk with matted hair. The best part came in the last scene when, with deft strokes of paint and some powder, Bimala turned herself into a bloated, pox-infected woman.

'How can you do that?' Neela marvelled.

Bimala smiled. 'It's not that difficult. You mix the skin-coloured paint with powder and let it crust up on your skin, like this. And then you add another layer of this reddish paint, and then some of this oily, oozy stuff. Wonderfully disgusting, isn't it? And then you stuff cotton wool into your cheeks, like this. Oh dear, there's my cue!'

And with that, Bimala rushed onstage.

It was late by the time the rehearsal, with all its slip-ups and laughter, was over. Neela sat in the back seat of Bimala's car, her heart speeding. All evening, she'd distracted herself with other things, but now there was no escaping the truth. In just a little while, she would be dropped off at the place specified in the note. Soon after that, the army lorry carrying the prisoners would arrive at the same spot. And then? *If all goes well, I'll have Baba back, she thought. And if not?* Neela shuddered violently and pushed the thought out of her mind. She couldn't bear to think of having to return home alone, and of the devastated look on Ma's face when she told her of her failure.

'Neela,' Bimala whispered in the dark, 'we're almost there. I have some things for you that might come in handy. Here's an old cotton frock of mine. It's a bit tattered, but it won't attract any attention. It has long sleeves and a collar. Why don't you put it on over the dress you're wearing.'

Silently, as the car sped through the emptied streets of Calcutta, Neela pulled the dowdy old frock over the lace-and-silk dress she'd worn to the Drama Club. She slipped off the shiny leather shoes and braided her hair once again into a tight, old-fashioned braid. Bimala was right—now she looked like any poor girl on a street corner that no one would look at twice.

'You think of everything, Bimala,' Neela said in admiration.

'I've put some food in the bundle,' Bimala said, 'and some money—enough to get you and your father home. I was told that Biren will have clothes for him. And here's a shawl, in case you get cold waiting out there. This packet is for Samar—I know he must be short of money, too. Tell him I'll be praying for him. And tell him to send me word whenever he can.' She wiped her eyes and cleared her throat. 'It's been fun having you here, and planning all this. I feel I'm part of something big, at least for a little while!' She paused, then said, 'I've kept the baoul's costume you wore when you arrived at our house, to remind me of that. I hope you don't mind.'

'Of course not. I don't know what I would have done without you. Thank you for everything.' Neela reached for Bimala's hand and squeezed it. 'Samar was right about you.'

'I hope I'll get a chance to see you again, some day.'

'I hope so, too,' Neela said, her voice a bit shaky.

The car came to a halt.

'Bimala memsahib, here's the place you wanted me to bring you to,' the driver said, his tone full of misgiving. 'It's in the middle of nowhere—not safe at all so late at night. If Master were to learn of this, for certain I would lose my job.'

'We'll be leaving in a minute,' Bimala assured him. She gave Neela a hug. 'Go and wait in the shadow of that big banyan tree on the corner. Bishu's probably waiting there, too. I'm sorry that I can't wait with you. But if I'm not back home right away, Papa will get suspicious.' She handed Neela the bundle. 'Oh, I put one more thing in there—my make-up box. Who knows, maybe it'll come in handy.'

Standing under the banyan tree, Neela watched the receding red tail lights of Bimala's car being swallowed up by blackness. There was total silence around her now. Neela felt as though she was the last living person left on earth. This was not a residential area, so there were no streetlamps nearby. And the faint light from a new moon only made the banyan shadows seem longer and darker. Where in heaven's name was Bishu?

'Bishu!' she called softly, then louder, trying to get her eyes used to the darkness. 'Bishu! Where are you?'

There was no reply.

Neela's hands were clammy with sweat as she clutched at the bundle. *What if this whole thing is a plot?* Neela thought. *What if that note wasn't from Samar at all? What if Bishu isn't the loyal servant Bimala believes him to be? Perhaps his plan is to kidnap me and sell me to slave traders.* Even back in her village, she had heard of things like that happening, of girls who disappeared, never to be heard from again.

There was a rustling sound behind her. Turning, Neela could see a shape creeping through the hanging roots of the banyan tree. Someone's shadow reached out, long and distorted, toward her.

The blood pounded in her head with fear—and anger. Whoever he was, he wouldn't take her without a fight! Before she could think her action through and grow too scared to move, she rushed at the shape and swung the bundle as hard as she could. It hit him in the belly, and with a grunt, he fell back.

'Stay away!' she yelled. 'Or I'll really hurt you next time.'

'Stop!' gasped her attacker. 'You've really hurt me already! I'm going to be black-and-blue all over tomorrow.' Then, surprisingly, he started to laugh.

His voice sounded familiar. Neela took a step toward him and peered into his face. It was Samar!

'You shouldn't creep up on a person like that!' she said angrily. 'You scared me almost to death!'

'I was trying to attract your attention silently, without alerting anyone,' he said with a smile. 'But I guess that wasn't to be! Thank God the lorry isn't here yet!'

'Where's Bishu?'

'He's helping me with the cart. See, over there—' Samar pointed.

A long, flat, two-wheeled cart, the kind often used in Neela's village, was in the middle of the narrow street, blocking the way. It was loaded with bundles and boxes of various sizes. Bishu was kneeling by it.

'What's he doing?' Neela asked.

'He's removing a wheel. That's going to be our story— yours and mine—that our cart broke down here, on our way back from the market, and it was too heavy for us to push out of the way. When the lorry stops—and it must, because it can't get past us—we're going to ask the soldiers for help. Be sure you look suitably scared! When the soldiers get down—well, Biren and his men should be waiting behind that warehouse on the other side of the road!'

'Are they there already?'

'I'm not sure. I came from another direction with the cart. I saw Bishu waiting here, and I asked him to give me a hand with the wheel.'

Bishu came up to them as they spoke. 'I'm done, Master Samar,' he said.

'Thank you, Bishu. You go on home now. In case things go wrong, you mustn't be found here.'

'But I—' Bishu started. Neela could see that he, too, wanted to be part of the rescue.

Samar shook his head. 'Bimala needs you,' he said. 'You must keep yourself safe for her sake.'

Bishu nodded reluctantly. In a moment he had faded into the darkness.

Then there was just the two of them, sitting on the lopsided cart, waiting. Neela stared intently at the dark hulk of the warehouse, but she could see no movement. She heard the mournful clang of a bell from some distant cathedral, echoing eerily. Eleven rings! In spite of herself, she shivered. In the dark, Samar's hand reached for hers. His fingers were sweaty, just as hers were. Somehow it made her feel a little better, knowing that he was nervous, too.

'It's time,' he whispered, and he gave her hand a small squeeze.

The Rescue Mission

It seemed to Neela that an age had passed since the bell had struck the hour. Its echoes had long since died away and been replaced by a thick silence. *Where is that lorry?* Neela wondered. Had they been given the wrong information? What if the driver had decided to take a different route to the docks? In that case, the freedom fighters would never be able to catch up with them. Neela felt a sob gathering in her throat, threatening to burst through her clamped lips. *Oh, Baba, where are you?* she thought. She glanced at Samar, but he was staring worriedly down the dark road, biting his knuckle.

Then they heard the roar of a heavy engine, reverberating through the night. In a moment, they saw the headlights of a covered lorry as it bumped its way across the potholes of the little street. Samar quickly stood up, yelling and waving his hands in the air. Neela waved, too. She longed to glance at the warehouse to see if the freedom fighters were in position, but she was afraid. One careless glance might give their presence away. And what if—this was a worse possibility—what if she looked, and no one was there?

Don't think bad-luck thoughts! she scolded herself. Besides, she had enough other things to worry about. The lorry was coming straight at them, very fast. Maybe the driver couldn't see them properly here in the dark. Maybe he'd see them—but too late—and would not be able to stop. Maybe he wouldn't even care to stop but would slam his way right through the cart, which was made only of flimsy bamboo poles. Neela stiffened and closed her eyes, expecting the huge vehicle to crash into her at any moment.

With a screech of brakes, the lorry came to a halt only a couple of feet away from them. An angry voice was yelling and cursing, ordering them to clear the road. Samar went up to the driver's window.

'Help us, please!' he shouted.

The driver, a large, bearded Indian in a turban, yelled and shook his fist at Samar, telling him to get out of the way. A British officer carrying a gun jumped down from where he was sitting on the other side.

'Please, sir!' Samar went up to him, bowing deferentially. 'My cousin and I are having trouble.' He pointed to Neela, who huddled against the cart, trying to shield her eyes from the glare of the truck's headlights. She tried to look suitably scared, as Samar had advised her. That part wasn't difficult! Her heart hammered in her chest as she watched the officer from behind her raised arm to see what he might do.

'Our cart has lost a wheel, sir,' Samar was explaining in broken English mixed with Bengali. 'We've been trying to move it, but we can't by ourselves. Could you please help us, sir?'

'Damn idiot natives!' shouted the officer. '*Suar ka baccha!* Children of swine! Couldn't you find some other place to break down? Do you realize that you're impeding His Majesty's business?' He swiped viciously with his gun at Samar, who ducked just in time.

'Havildar!' the officer yelled. 'Get a couple of men to push that stupid cart out of the road and into the ditch. Double quick!'

'Ji saab!' came a voice from the back. 'Right away, saab!' Someone barked orders, and four Indian soldiers jumped down from the truck and ran to the cart. Neela barely managed to step away from it before they dragged it to the ditch and tilted it over, along with everything on it. Neela cried out and lunged forward, trying to save some of the boxes, but one of the soldiers laughed and shoved her away roughly.

'Too late now, girl!' he snarled in Bengali. 'Out of our way, unless you want to end up in the ditch yourself!'

Neela stared in angry astonishment at the man in his khaki uniform. He was short and dark, with a curly moustache similar to the one that Ramdeen, who owned a stall in their village bazaar, had. Why, he was an Indian, a Bengali, just like her! How could he be so cruel to her, then? How could he slavishly obey a Britisher, no matter what the man commanded?

Behind her, she heard confused cries and yells. Whirling around, she saw that a number of dark figures had appeared on the scene. One of them, his nose and mouth covered by a scarf, held a gun to the back of the British officer's head.

'Drop your weapon,' he ordered.

Biren had arrived!

In just a few minutes, the freedom fighters, their faces blackened or wrapped in cloths, had taken the soldiers' weapons. 'Tie them up securely, arms and legs both,' Biren instructed.

The officer glared at him. 'You bloody terrorist!' he spluttered. 'Do you know who I am? I'm Major Lytton! You'll never get away with this! I'll see you hung!'

Biren gave a cool laugh. 'Oh, I forgot,' he said to his men. 'Be sure to gag them, too.'

'We should just shoot them and be rid of such trash!' one of the freedom fighters said heatedly.

Biren shook his head. 'Remember the vow we took? We hurt people if we must, but unnecessary killing is never our way.'

'What shall we do with them, then? We can't let passersby find them.'

'Since Major Lytton seems to like the ditch so much,' Biren said, 'let's roll them into it! The mud will keep them nice and cool, and they won't be found for quite a while. You—' he pointed to a lanky young man, and Neela realized he was being careful not to use any names. 'You know how to drive the lorry. Take the wheel. Men, I want just a handful of you on the truck. Keep the rifles with you. The rest should scatter—in case we get caught. You know where to meet up with us again. Let's get moving!'

He beckoned to Neela, who was watching him admiringly. 'Climb into the back, Sister, and help my men untie the prisoners. I think you might find someone special there!'

The back of the lorry, covered in canvas, was crowded, dark, and smelly with the odour of bodies that hadn't bathed in a long time. But Neela didn't mind. Armed with the knife she'd been given, she went from one man to another, cutting their bonds and giving them water from a canteen. The men blessed her and drank deeply.

'Thank you, Daughter!' they said as they splashed the cool water on their grimy faces.

But none of them was her father. Neela's heart sank as she made her way through the lorry, which had started moving. *Was Biren mistaken? Was there maybe another group of prisoners, on another lorry, that we missed?* She was glad that all the men on this truck were freed, but still her eyes filled with tears of disappointment.

She had almost reached the front end of the lorry when she saw a man sitting on the floor, half-hidden behind two other prisoners. His bandaged head rested wearily against the lorry's side. His eyes were closed, and his gaunt face was half-covered by an untidy, grizzly beard. But Neela knew him right away.

'Baba!' she cried, pushing through the crowd of bodies.

The man opened his eyes and stared incredulously at her. Then he shook his head and rubbed his eyes. 'I must be delirious again,' he muttered to himself.

'No, Baba,' Neela said as she flung herself into his arms. 'It's really me, Neela!'

For a long moment Hari Charan said nothing. He just held his daughter close and seemed to breathe in the smell of her hair. Neela could feel his arms trembling. Finally, he wiped his eyes and said, 'God is great indeed! I had given up all hope of freedom, or of seeing you and your mother.' Then, with a frown, he asked, 'How did you get here?'

Eagerly, Neela started to tell her father all the things that had happened to her since he had left home. She was so excited that at times her words got tangled up in her mouth, and Hari Charan, smiling, had to tell her to slow down. But finally she'd given her father the gist of the story.

'There's so much more—I'll have to tell you some other time about Bimala and her papa, and Bishu, and the girls at the Drama Club, and how Samar dressed up as the monkey-dance man! And how scared I was when I was waiting in the road for the truck,' she ended. Then she looked at her father anxiously. 'I hope you're not angry with me for running away from home? I knew Ma would worry, but I didn't know how else to help you.'

Hari Charan shook his head and gave her a warm hug. 'How can I be angry? If it wasn't for you, I'd be deported by now, to spend the rest of my life away from India and my family. You were a smart, brave girl to do what you did, and I think your mother will understand.' Then he tried to make his face stern. 'You'd better not make a habit of it, though, or I might have to give you a spanking, like your mother's always asking me to!'

'Yes, Baba!' Neela said meekly.

They both burst out laughing.

Suddenly the lorry came to a stop. The canvas covering the back was lifted, and Biren climbed up. The freed prisoners crowded around him. The younger men touched his feet to show respect. Hari Charan grasped Biren's hands in his.

'You've saved our lives!' he said. 'How can we ever thank you?'

'No need for thanks,' Biren said. 'I'm happy that, by luck and God's grace, I was able to do it. It'll be a great blow to British pride—capturing back their prisoners from under their noses!' He tousled Neela's hair. 'You have quite a daughter! She's the one who gave me the idea!'

Neela smiled at Biren.

'But listen carefully—we have no time to lose,' Biren continued. 'By now, soldiers at the ship must have realized what has happened, and they will have sounded an alarm. We must get out of Calcutta right away—the army will be looking for this lorry. We're going to drive it to one of our centres up north. Our people there are so good at changing the appearance of a vehicle that not even its own mother would recognize it! Those of you who want to come with us and join in our fight are welcome to. For the rest, this is where we must say good-bye.'

Several of the younger men decided to go with Biren,

while others opted to return home or go back to the Congress Party.

'We're near Howrah Station,' Biren told them. 'You'll be able to catch a train or a bus quite easily to wherever you want to go. We have some clothes here for you, so you can change out of your prison garb. You must separate from each other right away—the police are sure to be searching, and they'll be more suspicious of groups of men than of individuals.'

While the men changed hurriedly in the truck, Neela climbed down and looked around her. In the light of a streetlamp, she recognized the Howrah Bridge, looming in the distance. If they could just cross it and get onto a train for Shona Gram! Then she saw Hari Charan being helped off the truck. He had a bad limp and walked very slowly. He grimaced in pain as he leaned on one of his companions.

Neela ran to him, her heart sinking. 'What's wrong, Baba?' she asked anxiously.

'A policeman hit my shin with a lathi during the march,' he told her. 'May have broken something. The pain's better now, but I don't think the bone's healed right.'

Neela's eyes filled with tears of despair. She knew he'd never be able to walk in this condition.

Biren watched them for a moment. Then he beckoned to Samar.

'They could do with some help,' he said. 'Go with them as far as their village. Then come back to our centre in Calcutta and wait there for your next assignment.'

The driver revved the engine.

'*Vande Mataram*!' Biren shouted, his arm upraised.

'*Vande Mataram*!' everyone responded.

'Great success to you!'

'See you under the tricoloured flag!'

'Goddess Kali bless you!'

'Victory for India!'

Then, in a cloud of dust, the freedom fighters were gone.

Unexpected Obstacles

Slowly, unsteadily, the three of them made their way across the bridge. Hari Charan leaned heavily on Samar, who took much of the older man's weight, but once in a while Samar stumbled in the dim lighting, and Hari Charan gasped as his injured leg hit the ground. Neela walked behind them, carrying her bundle and feeling useless. If only she could do something to take away her father's pain!

'We're almost there now,' Samar whispered encouragingly. 'See, there's the main entrance to the station. It's bound to be fairly empty at this time of night. I'll set you down on a bench and go and get our tickets— and then we'll be on a train to Shona Gram before you know it!'

But as they neared the station, Neela thought something didn't seem right. Had those tall, metal gates been there the first time she'd been at the station?

'Oh no,' said Samar in dismay. 'They've shut the gates and bolted them! What on earth is going on?'

They looked around them wildly. The sidewalks outside

the station were empty at this time of night; the vendors had all gone home. Only a few beggars still huddled in their rags under the scant cover provided by the far end of the station wall. No, there was someone else—the night watchman! They could hear the stomp of his boots as he walked up and down, banging his lathi on the cobbles and crying, 'Hoshiar! Careful! Who goes there?'

Neela tensed. 'Did he see us?' she asked Samar.

He shook his head. 'I think that's just what he says over and over. Listen!'

'Hoshiar!' The cry was muted now as the watchman turned the corner, moving away.

'Let's hurry and get under cover of the wall's darkness,' Samar said. 'Maybe one of the beggars can tell us what's happening.'

They lowered themselves onto the concrete pavement near one of the huddled groups of beggars, who watched them in wary suspicion. But when Samar explained to them that he was taking his sick uncle back to his village home, they grew a little friendlier. They told Samar that for the past week or so, all night trains had been stopped because of the activities of freedom fighters. The station was kept locked from midnight to six a.m. The morning trains would start running only after that.

'After six a.m.?' Samar's voice was worried. 'That's a long wait.' Neela couldn't see his expression in the dark, but she knew what he must be thinking. By six a.m., the authorities would know that the prisoners had been freed, and a massive search would begin. How would they, handicapped as they were by Hari Charan's injury, avoid the soldiers?

Hari Charan must have been thinking along the same lines, because he tugged at Samar's kurta. When the boy leaned down, he whispered, 'Leave me here with the beggars for a day or two—I think I'll be safe enough. Smear a little more dirt on my clothes, slash them in a couple of places, and I'll look just like them. Neela should go home tomorrow, and you should go back to the centre. I'll make my way to Shona Gram on my own in a couple of days, when the search is over.'

'Never!' Neela cried. 'I'm not leaving you again, no matter what. They're sure to catch you, especially with that bandage on your head. And even if no one caught you, ill as you are, you wouldn't be able to get on the train by yourself.' She draped the shawl Bimala had given her protectively around her father.

Samar nodded his head. 'Neela's right, sir,' he said. 'We can't just leave you, not after all the trouble we've taken to rescue you! Let's try to get some rest now. In the morning, I'll go into the station and check out the situation.'

They ate a few mouthfuls of the food Bimala had packed for them.

'Luchis! With fried eggplant!' Hari Charan said appreciatively. 'Why, I haven't eaten so well since Usha's wedding! What a splendid young lady your cousin is!'

'I'll pass on the compliment,' Samar said with a grin. 'Though I'm afraid it'll go straight to her head, and there'll be no talking to her after that!'

Neela smiled wanly. She was too exhausted even to

laugh. The day's tensions had worn her out, but she was too wound up to sleep. She dozed fitfully, starting at the strange night sounds all around her. When she finally did manage to fall asleep, it was only to be jerked awake by the screeching brakes of a bus that came to a halt near them. She was surprised to see it was morning. Vendors were already setting up their wares, and passengers had started to arrive. But where was Samar?

'He went into the station to try to get tickets,' Hari Charan said, noting the anxious look on her face, 'Don't worry!'

But Neela couldn't help worrying. *Why didn't he wake me before going off?* she thought angrily. *How long has he been gone? What if there are police inside? What if they've caught him and identified him as one of the freedom fighters involved in last night's rescue mission? What if they've tortured him until he broke and confessed? What if the police are coming to get Baba and me, right now?*

A hand fell on her shoulder, causing her to jump with a small scream.

'Neela, come on!' Jubilation sounded in Samar's whisper. 'I've got the tickets.'

They decided that Neela and Hari Charan would walk in separately and meet Samar on Platform Four. There, a train that would pass by Shona Gram on its way to Bardhaman was already waiting.

'It would look more natural this way,' Samar said. 'You know, just a regular father and daughter, going some place together. Here are your tickets. Let's wrap the shawl around you carefully, sir, so the bandage doesn't show. Neela, can you manage?'

Neela nodded, not wasting her energy on words. She gritted her teeth and took on as much of her father's weight as she could. Together they staggered toward Platform Four—and towards freedom!

Fortunately, the train wasn't crowded. They settled themselves in the very last compartment, which was empty. The train lurched to a start.

Samar breathed a sigh of relief. 'We made it! There were a lot of policemen hanging around near the ticket counters, asking questions. They stopped me, too. I'd already bought my tickets by then. I stammered and acted half-witted, and I told them that I was going to see a sick mother in Bardhaman. Luckily, they didn't check how many tickets I had, or where they were for.'

'You would have been in big trouble if they had,' Neela said, her heart beating fast. 'They could have put you in jail, if they had gotten suspicious.'

'Who c-c-could suspect poor Sh-sh-shomu?' Samar stuttered. All of a sudden, there was a vacant, cross-eyed expression on his face—so convincing that Neela drew in her breath in shock.

'P-p-pretty lady give two paise to Sh-sh-sh—?' he continued through slack lips.

'Did the freedom fighters teach you how to act like that?' Neela asked, fascinated.

'Teach me? This is natural talent, I'd like you to know, young miss.' Samar drew himself up to his full height, pretending to be offended.

Neela burst out in laughter. She glanced at her father to see if he found Samar as funny as she did, but he was gazing somberly out the window at the rice fields speeding by.

'You're very quiet, Baba,' she said, watching him with a concerned frown.

'Ah, my dear,' he said, 'there's so much that has happened to me recently. It's turned my life around. I'm just trying to figure out the new me, and what he thinks.'

'Like what?'

'When I came to Calcutta, I contacted the Bengal branch of the Congress Party, saying I wanted to take part in their Quit India march. I met a number of really fine people there. I learned so much about the freedom struggle going on all over the country. Some of them had taken part in the Salt March with Gandhiji—'

'The Salt March?' asked Neela. Beside her, she could sense Samar listening, too.

'Yes! Gandhiji—they call him Bapu, father of the nation—says that the British have no right to tax Indians for salt. It comes out of the Indian Ocean, and every Indian has a right to it. So he marched to the ocean with a lot of his followers, made some salt, and took it for his use— and he said that every Indian should do so, too. As you can imagine, the British were upset—a lot of arrests were made. But Gandhiji was insistent that his people not fight back physically. He says that we—the Indian people—

will win over the British the right way, through non-violence.'

Neela nodded. She liked what she heard of this Gandhiji.

'But that's nonsense,' Samar burst out. 'The British will never hand India back to us unless we make them!'

'Yes, that's true,' Hari Charan said. 'But non-violence—civil disobedience, Gandhiji calls it—is the best and strongest strategy against them. Not only will we have right on our side, but the whole world will see that we do. They'll see the villainy of the British, and they'll shame them into setting us free.'

'Fah! The British have no shame!' Samar said.

'But Gandhiji is a great leader, you have to agree,' Hari Charan said. 'No wonder he's called Mahatma, Great Soul. He's dedicated his whole life to the people of India—'

'So has Netaji Subhash Bose,' Samar interrupted. 'And his way, fighting the British with their own fire, killing their leaders until they all get the message and leave—is more effective!' He slammed his fist down on the bench to stress his point.

Hari Charan shook his head. 'I don't know. One of my cellmates in prison had read a lot of Gandhiji's writings. He used to quote from them from time to time. Gandhiji says, "An eye for an eye leaves the whole world blind." That makes a lot of sense to me.'

Neela looked from her father's face to Samar's. It was obvious that they weren't going to agree. It distressed her because she cared so much for them both. Personally, she thought Gandhiji's peaceful way was a better one. But she could see why Netaji's way—and Biren's—would appeal more to many, and especially to younger people who wanted independence right away. And his belief— to give one's life for one's motherland—was very heroic and attractive. Neela felt tired and confused. There were so many conflicts in the world, so many choices to make. It was difficult to know what was right.

The train had stopped at a fairly large station, and they looked out the windows at the platform, where people were milling around, carrying baskets of vegetables, eggs, and fish.

'We're already at Shaluk Para,' Hari Charan said. 'There's a big market at Jal Gram, not too far from here. But it's on another rail line. That's why all these men are at the station, I guess. They're probably waiting to take the connecting train.'

Jal Gram! The name filled Neela with guilty memories of the day before she ran away from home. She would have to tell Baba—and soon, before Ma did—about the nice lady who wanted her to get engaged to her son! Neela hoped Baba would understand why she wasn't ready for such a big step yet.

'Strange!' muttered Samar, craning his neck out of the farthest window. 'No one seems to be getting off our train. And those men in khaki, pushing through the crowd— could they be the police? I'd better go take a look.'

Neela and her father watched him slip out the door.

'He's a good boy,' Hari Charan said, half to himself. 'Brave and intelligent—and unselfish, too.'

Through her fear, Neela's heart leaped in pleasure to hear her father praise Samar.

'As are you, my child.' Hari Charan turned to her. 'I hope you'll help me when we get back home. I have all kinds of plans about educating the villagers about what's really going on in the country. We must all support the battle for independence, one way or another.'

'Of course I will!' Neela said, surprised and pleased. She felt proud that her father considered her grown up enough to help him with such an important job. 'I'd love to! I'll do whatever you—!'

At that moment, Samar burst into the compartment. His face was tense.

Neela stared at him. Her mouth felt dry and chalky.

'Constables,' Samar panted. 'A whole company of them! Someone told me they're already on the train. They're searching all the passengers. No one is allowed to leave the train until they've checked everyone.'

With a shrill whistle and a lurch, the train started on its way again. Its rocking motion hadn't bothered Neela before, but now she felt nauseous. And scared. What would happen to them?

Beside her, Samar and Hari Charan were trying to figure out a plan. Neela, too, tried to think of something to help them.

'Neela—we must save her, at least!' Hari Charan said. 'They mustn't realize she's with us. Neela, I want you to go to another compartment right now, you hear me? I noticed a jenana compartment, just for women, on the other side of the toilet. I want you to—'

Neela shook her head. 'I'm not leaving you!'

'Don't be stubborn!' her father said angrily. 'You've got to go, and now!'

Samar was looking at the wall. Up near the ceiling, there was a scarlet sign. It read, *To Stop Train, Pull Chain.* There was a chain with a scarlet handle hanging next to it.

'What if I pull the chain?' he said. 'The train will stop, and then maybe we can hurry down and hide in the fields while the constables are still at the other end of the train. I know some good camouflage tricks. We can get away, I think.'

Hari Charan shook his head. 'I won't be able to do it, not with this leg. But it's a good idea. You can do it— you're young and fast—you'll be able to outrun the constables, if you need to. I think you should go ahead! After you put Neela in the jenana compartment, that is.'

'I can't abandon you like that,' Samar said.

'You must!' Hari Charan insisted. 'I appreciate your loyalty, but there's no point in all of us ending up in jail, is there?'

Neela looked around desperately. There seemed no way out. *What would happen when the constables searched Baba and found the wound on his head? And Samar, too, must have a big scar from his earlier injury.*

The constables would probably arrest them both on the spot. Oh, to have worked so hard and to be so close to home and freedom—only to have it snatched away like this! It's not fair! She gripped the bundle she was holding on her knee and gave it an angry shake.

Something rattled inside. It was the make-up box.

Hari Charan and Samar were still arguing about what to do.

Neela shook her father's arm.

'Listen to me,' she said. 'I have an idea.'

When the head constable walked into the last compartment, he was in a foul mood. He and his men had spent an hour searching the train and had found no one except foolish peasants with smelly baskets of fish and terrified village families with equally smelly infants. The informant—a shifty-eyed guy who'd shown up outside the police station this morning—who had told them about a group of terrorists being on the train was wrong. Or had he done it on purpose? You couldn't even trust traitors these days! What was the world coming to? Well, that informant was going to be sore and sorry if he, the head constable, ever saw him again. Unless this last compartment yielded something valuable.

Looking in, the constable saw that the compartment held only three people. One of these was a lanky girl in a ragged, dirty frock. He dismissed her right away. Across from her sat a young man who looked like he was crazed in the head. He drooled and pointed at things outside the window and talked to himself. Every once in a while he slapped himself in the face. That didn't look like the kind of person they were looking for either.

Next to the girl lay a man, covered up in a shawl, shivering and moaning. Now, that looked suspicious! Why would he be lying down, all covered up like that, unless he had something to hide? The moaning was probably just an act. And anyone could pretend to shiver! The head constable yelled at one of his men to snatch the cover off the man.

But the girl was standing up, bowing deferentially.

'Oh sir, oh respected Inspector saab,' she cried. 'Thank God you are here! Please help us!'

The head constable smiled. He liked being called Inspector saab, though he wasn't quite an inspector yet. The girl seemed polite and respectful enough, so he asked her, less gruffly than usual, what the matter was.

'We got on three stations ago, saab. It's my poor father, saab. I'm taking him to the hospital in Bardhaman. Maybe you can send one of your men along with us, to help? As you can see, I have only my cousin with me, and he's weak in the brain, not much of a help at all—'

The head constable pointed to her father with his lathi. 'What's wrong with him?'

'Four days ago, he started having a terrible fever, and then yesterday red boils broke out all over him—'

The head constable took a step back toward the compartment door—and so did his men.

'They're full of pus, and now they've started to burst!'

The girl wrung her hands. 'Baba says the pain is terrible. And the itching! Sometimes he scratches himself till blood comes—see his right hand here—' The girl raised a corner of the shawl to show the constables a hand covered in boils and crusted with pus. It looked disgusting.

'The pox!' whispered one of the other constables. The men backed out of the door as fast as they could. The head constable backed out, too, holding a handkerchief over his nose and mouth.

'His face is even worse,' the girl said. 'Please look, Inspector saab.' She made a motion as though to pull the shawl off her father's head. He shivered and moaned more loudly.

'Stop, you idiot girl!' the head constable shouted. 'Your father has smallpox! You're all probably infected with it! I hope to God you haven't infected us, too. I want you off the train right away—Bansi, pull the chain in the next compartment!'

'Ji saab!' someone shouted. There was the sound of an alarm ringing. Jerkily, the train began to slow down.

'But, honourable saab, what will I do if you leave us down in the fields, in the middle of nowhere, with such a sick man?' Neela cried desperately, on the verge of tears.

'That's your problem, girl!' the head constable spat. 'There, the train has stopped—now get out! As soon as I leave the compartment, that is. Bansi, make sure they get off the train! And then cordon off this compartment. You, Montu, get me hot water, soap, and a clean towel—I've got to wash off all these germs.'

'Ji saab,' Bansi and Montu chorused unhappily.

Handkerchief pressed to his face, the head constable hurried down the corridor, cursing at his men to move faster. Bansi barely waited until he saw Neela and Samar shouldering Hari Charan's weight—fortunately, the man was still covered by the shawl. Then he, too, made his way as fast as he could down the corridor.

Neela, Hari Charan, and Samar sat in a field of mustard flowers, watching the train disappear around a grove of jackfruit trees. When it was gone, Samar fell back onto a bed of flowers, sighing with relief. 'I'm worn out with worrying!' he said. 'I must confess I didn't think we could pull it off! But you were great, Neela! Where did you learn to apply make-up like that? Maybe you could join our freedom fighters group.'

At the look on Hari Charan's face, he raised his hand hastily. 'Only joking, sir! You do look quite ghastly, by the way.'

Neela used a corner of the shawl and brushed some of the make-up from Hari Charan's face and right hand, which was all she'd had time to work on.

'I was so scared that the constable would want to see Baba's whole body—or even his entire arm!' she said. 'We were very lucky.'

'Lucky, yes,' her father said, 'but you were also brave and quick-witted. That's really what saved us!' He patted her head. 'I'm proud of you, Daughter, and so will your mother be, when I tell her.'

Neela beamed. Suddenly, she couldn't wait to see her mother.

'How far is it to your home from here?' Samar asked.

'Only a mile or so,' Hari Charan said. He pointed. 'The village starts right beyond that jackfruit grove. There's a shortcut, too, past the weavers' huts.'

'Do you think you can make it on your own? It's better if I'm not seen by the villagers.'

Hari Charan nodded. 'Neela can help me from here on.' He clasped Samar's hands in both of his. 'Thank you so much! I wish you the best with your future plans, whatever you choose to do, and I'm sure Neela wishes you the same. Be safe!'

'Good-bye, Neela,' Samar said. He was looking at her intently. There was so much Neela wanted to tell him— but a huge lump of shyness seemed to block her throat.

'Thank you for everything,' she finally managed to whisper. 'Come and see us when you can.'

'If I'm alive, I will!' Samar said.

The simple words struck Neela like a blow. Neither of them knew what dangers lurked in his future. Would he live long enough to see a free India? Would he really be able to come back to Shona Gram?

Samar paused, as though he were waiting for Neela to say something else. When she didn't, he turned and started walking along the rail lines.

Neela was furious with herself. Now she'd never get a chance to tell him what she had wanted to say: How he'd been her truest friend and had comforted her in moments of fear. How he'd helped her grow, so that she was

returning to the village a stronger person. And finally—
how much she liked him!

A thought came to her. '*Vande Mataram!*' she sang.

You are the strength in our arms, Mother.
You are the devotion in our heart.
We worship you! We worship you!
We worship you throughout the land!

In the distance, Samar stopped walking. Turning, he
listened to the lilting, beautiful notes, to the inspiring words
of the song. It seemed to Neela that he heard what was
under the words as well—all the things left unspoken in
her heart. When the song ended, he raised his hand.

'Thank you for that,' he shouted. 'Don't worry. I'll be
careful. And I'll come back! *Vande Mataram!*'

Neela and her father watched as Samar's figure grew
smaller and smaller and finally disappeared into the fields.
Then Hari Charan put his arm around his daughter.

'Come on, *shona*,' he said. 'Samar's a smart boy. He'll
survive whatever challenges life sets down in front of him.
I have a feeling we'll be seeing more of him—maybe
sooner than we think. Meanwhile, we have a lot to do!'

'Yes, Baba,' Neela said. 'We certainly have!' The song
had filled her with a sense of hope and purpose. Whatever
the future held wasn't in her control. But for now, she'd
do what she could to be a small part of the big work that

was going on around them.

The two of them began to make their slow way homeward, through the golden mustard fields.

'You know, Baba,' Neela said as she looked around her, 'until I went away, I didn't realize how beautiful our village is. There are so many different colours all around us—the dark green of the mango leaves, the bright green of the banana trees, the silvery-blue ponds, even the rich reddish-brown of the mud we're walking on!'

'And don't forget the gold of the mustard flowers,' her father said. 'That's what Shona Gram is named for!'

Neela supported her father as they made their way in companionable silence. Looking up at the sky, she marvelled at all the shapes in the clouds—elephants, palaces, peacocks—and wasn't that a woman, a beautiful woman, like the one who appeared in her dreams? Only she seemed to be glittering with smiles on this sunny afternoon. Maybe she was the motherland, looking down on Neela, blessing her.

'Baba, look!' Neela started to say. But already the clouds had shifted.

Suddenly her father gripped her shoulder tightly and stood very still. There was a clearing in the grove of bamboos ahead of them—and through it Neela could see their house. And that woman—could that be Neela's beautiful mother, dressed in a torn, old sari, as though she didn't care anymore what she looked like—tethering Budhi to a tree?

'Ma!' Neela shouted. 'It's us! I've brought Baba back!'

The woman looked up. *Yes, it was Ma!* Neela watched

as her mother's thin face broke into an incredulous smile when she spotted her daughter and her husband. She began to run toward them. Budhi, who hadn't been tied up properly, came gambolling, too, mooing so loudly that it was a wonder all the neighbours didn't run out to see what was going on.

Neela broke into a run herself, not stopping until she had thrown herself into her mother's arms. She burrowed her face into her mother's neck. How much she had missed her! And how many stories she had for her! What would Sarada think of the way her daughter had changed and grown? And the baoul? What would he think? For she must tell him of her adventures when he came around again—and soon, she hoped.

But for now it was enough to draw in a deep breath and be aware of her mother's hands in her hair. To smell her mother's skin, that distinctive mix of cooking spices and sandalwood soap Neela had loved since she was a baby. To feel Budhi butting her side impatiently as she tried to squeeze between mother and daughter. To sense the smile on her father's face as he watched the whole scene from the edge of the bamboo grove.

'Oh, Ma,' Neela whispered, 'I'm so happy to be home!'